BENEATH

THE

WATCHER TREE

Illustrations by Daria Zaltur

Cover design by: Irfan B.

Proofreading and editing by Deb Hall with The Write Insight (thewriteinsight.com).

NOTE FROM THE AUTHOR

I have wanted to write a children's book for years, but I wasn't sure what kind of children's book I wanted it to be. Now I know—a cute, cozy mystery series that both adults and children can enjoy.

There's mischief, there's marshmallows, and there's the magical quality of the unknown and the what-might-be (only without the magic.)

If you've picked this book up for your child, you can rest in the knowledge that it is Christian, it is clean, and it is filled with valuable lessons. There might be a few moments in this book that will spark your child to come ask you a question for clarification. Be prepared!

The best thing about this book (and the upcoming series) is that I now have four amazing nephews and two wonderful nieces to share them with. I hope you and your little ones have as much fun reading them as I am writing them.

With love,
C.C. Warrens

WORDS THAT MAY BE NEW TO YOU

Oma (Oh-ma): German for Grandma
Opa (Oh-pa): German for Grandpa
Liebling (Lee-bling): German for Darling
Quirk (kwerk): move or twist- usually to the side.
Scallywaggle (scally – waggle): Holly's version of
        "scallywag," which means someone who
        behaves in a mischievous way.
Mischief (miss-chiff): playful misbehavior.
        Mischievous (miss-chiff-us.)

BENEATH

THE

WATCHER TREE

STONY BROOKE, KANSAS

1998

Carrot-red hair swishing behind her like a superhero cape, nine-year-old Holly shot out the back door of the house and leaped off the porch. The wind snatched at the dress she wore over her leggings, but not enough to help her fly. She landed in the yard with a clumsy tuck and roll, and then popped to her feet.

She made a beeline for the woods, Mom's voice snapping after her. "Holly Marie Cross, you come back here!"

Come back and pose for pictures like a doll? Not a chance. There were adventures waiting. Dirty, exciting, unexpected adventures.

Her sister, Gin, was the twin who enjoyed posing for the camera. Holly was "something else." At least that was what Mom said when she put her hands on her hips and shook her head at her. Holly liked being something

1

else. She could be a pirate, a treasure hunter, a scallywaggle.

She tore through the woods, bounding over familiar roots and skirting around brush. These were her woods—she played in them every day—and she recognized every lumpy trunk she could climb and every low-hanging limb she could swing from.

As she rounded an old pine, she smacked into something that shouldn't be there—a person—and the two of them crashed to the ground like an overbalanced swing set.

Holly landed on top of the person with an *oomph,* the frilly bottom of her dress flying up over her head. She swatted it back down and brushed the tangled curtain of hair from her face.

The blond-haired, blue-eyed boy beneath her let out a groan and pushed at her shoulders. "Get off me, Holly."

She'd flattened Jordan, her best friend.

Stumbling upright, she took one of his hands and tried to heave him to his feet, but he was too heavy. He was a year older and a lot bigger than she was, but she would catch up someday. She was sure of that.

"Were you pretending to be a tree?" she asked when he pushed himself up. It was certainly the place to be a tree.

"No, I was watching a squirrel." He brushed a leaf from his hair and looked over her clothes. "Why do you look so pretty today?"

Holly drew herself up, insulted. "Take that back."

Jordan ducked his head and scuffed a shoe in the dirt. "Maybe I don't wanna take it back."

She scowled and folded her arms. "Mom was taking summer pictures. I couldn't sit still anymore. My legs were gonna run away without me."

"That would be a story to tell." Jordan's dimples deepened with his grin. "I thought we could go treasure hunting. And Oma made fresh chocolate chip cookies. We could stop by her place after."

Ooh, cookies.

Holly's annoyance disappeared like a rabbit down a hole. She liked cookies. Oma, Jordan's grandma, was always baking something, and she shared her sweets as freely as she shared exciting stories.

"Well, I guess I forgive you. Come on." She grabbed his hand and dragged him through the woods toward one of their favorite places—the clearing. Campers and teenagers left all kinds of treasures behind. Someone had been camping there last week, so there was no telling what they might find.

Holly had found a broken, engraved bracelet there once. She loved it so much that Jordan did yard work all last summer so he could afford to buy her one for

Christmas. It even had her name on it, and she wore it every day.

It made her feel sort of girly and pretty. Not that she would ever tell *him* that.

At the sound of voices, Jordan slunk behind a tree, and Holly crowded in next to him, stepping on his foot.

"Sorry," she mouthed.

They peeked around the sides of the tree at the clearing. Older, bigger kids hung around, joking and laughing.

Colton, Mike, and Dan—fifth graders.

Holly's nose wrinkled. With fewer than fifteen hundred residents, the isolated town of Stony Brooke had few students and even fewer teachers. Multiple grades were crammed into one large classroom, with one teacher monitoring the book work. These three troublemakers always sat in the back row.

They enjoyed picking on younger kids. More than once, Colton had taunted Gin about the fact that she was mentally slower than everyone else.

Gin and Holly might be physically identical, but something went sideways when Gin was born, and her mind couldn't keep up with everyone else's. She had a special teacher for school.

Jordan's voice shook as he whispered, "We should go before they see us. Mike really doesn't like me."

Holly didn't want to tuck her tail and run off like a scared puppy, but she was half the size of the boys in the clearing. They wouldn't come after her because she was a girl, but if they decided to use Jordan as a piñata, there wasn't much she could do to protect him.

"Okay," she agreed.

Treasure hunting would have to wait.

As they backed away from the clearing, Dan, who had more freckles than strawberries had seeds, spotted them. He smacked the arms of his friends and pointed. "We've got runts."

"You mean *rats*," Mike said, meanness glittering in his dark eyes. "That's Sheriff Radcliffe's boy. Hey, *Rat*cliffe."

Holly stepped in front of Jordan, anger bubbling up. "He's my friend. You can't talk to him like that."

"What are you gonna do about it, runt?" Mike taunted.

Holly scooped up one of the pinecones from the ground by her feet and threw it at Mike. The pinecone plopped in the dirt, feet away from him, and the three fifth graders laughed. She picked up a couple more to throw. She would hit one of them before her arms got tired, and that would teach them to be nicer.

Jordan caught her arm after she hurled a second pinecone with all her strength. "You're gonna make them madder, Holly."

Mike grabbed a rock and tossed it up and down in his hand. "I think it's time for some dodgeball. Wanna play, rat boy?"

"Time to go." Holly dropped the pinecones and snagged Jordan's hand, yanking him behind her as she broke into a run. He stumbled over his too-big feet before catching up.

Holly breezed through the woods like a dart through air, aiming for one of the ancient pine trees. She slipped in between the thick, drooping branches and pulled Jordan with her, burrowing in deep.

They huddled close, hearts pounding in their chests, as the fifth graders crunched closer. Mike wasn't joking about playing dodgeball with rocks—he was mean all the way to his little toe—and he tossed the rock up and down in his hand.

"Rat-cliffe's dad locked my dad in the jail for no reason this past Christmas," Mike said. "If we find him, he's gonna be sorry."

Jordan's hand grew sweaty in Holly's, and she looked up at his frightened face. She wouldn't let them hurt her friend. She would fight them all by herself if she had to.

"At least he let your dad go. Mine's in prison," Colton grumbled. "Mom says he's never coming back."

The boys kept walking and calling for the "little rats." Holly waited until she couldn't hear them anymore before releasing Jordan's hand and inching forward, being as quiet as she was when she snuck downstairs for snacks in the middle of the night.

She peeked through the branches, searching, but they were alone in the woods. "I think it's okay to come out now."

"Good, 'cause I think I have Christmas tree in my mouth." Jordan spat as he followed her out of their hiding place.

Holly felt sticky all over from tree sap, and she peeled a piece of hair from her forehead and another from her neck. "Do you think we should tell your dad they wanna hurt you?"

Jordan shook his head. "No, he'll tell me to stand up to them, but I can't. There's too many of them, and they're too big."

Holly lifted her chin. "I won't let them hurt you."

"Thanks."

She squinted in the direction of the clearing. "Why do you think they were in our treasure hunting spot?"

"Probably smoking some weeds."

"Why would anyone smoke weeds?"

Jordan shrugged. "I don't know. It's something I heard my dad say when he got home from work one night. Something people do that they're not supposed to or something."

Jordan's dad was the town sheriff, and he probably came home with all kinds of interesting stories.

Holly wished she could be a fly on the wall of their living room when he shared them. But like a firefly, not a *fly* fly. Flies were gross and annoying.

"Should we go back to the clearing?" Jordan asked.

"No, let's dig around here. See if there's anything interesting." Holly toed the ground with her shiny black dress shoes.

"Isn't your mom gonna be mad if you get your dress dirty?"

Holly frowned down at the flowery outfit. "Yeah." But she couldn't help that. Mom should know not to dress her up in this silly stuff by now. She liked flowers and sparkles and purple things, but only in her bedroom, not on her body. They were too hard to play in.

Jordan shrugged one side of his book bag from his shoulder and unzipped it. "I borrowed Oma's garden tools."

"Perfect." Holly took one of the miniature shovels and wandered around, looking for the perfect spot.

"Is your dad at the bookstore today?" Jordan asked, digging into the ground where he'd been standing.

"Yeah."

Her and Gin's dad owned the local bookstore, Criss Cross Books. It was one of Holly's favorite places in the whole world. She loved going on adventures while sitting in a cozy chair with Dad and Gin.

She hoped she would someday stumble across actual treasure or a magical land like the kids in her books, but no matter how many times she opened and closed her closet door, Narnia never appeared.

"What's *your* dad doing today?" she asked.

"Working on the shed in the backyard."

"You didn't wanna help?"

Jordan shrugged. "I asked if I could, but he said I would get in the way."

The hurt in his eyes made Holly angry and sad all at once. "Well, I'm glad you're here with me, 'cause treasure hunting is no fun alone."

Holly's parents trusted Sheriff Radcliffe, but Holly didn't think he was a good dad. He never seemed to have time for Jordan, and if her dad was like that, it would make her sad.

Jordan offered her a half smile. "I'm glad you're my friend, Holly."

"Me too." Holly found a spot and knelt down, jamming the shovel into the dirt.

"Hey, here's something." Jordan dug his fingers into the hole he'd made and plucked out a piece of plastic. "Nope. Candy wrapper."

"And not even a good one." Who ate Butterfingers?

"I brought a trash bag." Jordan tugged a plastic grocery bag from his backpack so they could pick up any trash they found along the way. It was always tricking

9

them into thinking they found something good when they didn't. It was better to get rid of it.

Holly dug her shovel in deep for more dirt, and the tip hit something hard. She gasped. "I think I found something."

"Another candy wrapper or a tree root?"

Holly brushed the dirt off the object with her fingers, and sunlight sparkled off a grungy metal box. "Jordan, look!"

"Wow." He dropped his shovel and crouch-walked to her side. "Real buried treasure."

They both dug at the dirt with their bare hands until they could lift the box out. Holly set it on the ground and wiped her muddy fingers on her leggings. "So cool."

"Should we open it here?"

Holly looked over at him, but her answer caught in her throat. The tree she was digging near looked familiar, and a slithery feeling in her stomach told her they shouldn't be here.

She pushed to her feet and walked around the tree, her fingers and toes going cold when she realized she'd been digging between the roots on the back side of the watcher tree.

There were only two trees in all of Stony Brooke she avoided: the dead one near her house that she fell out of last summer, and the watcher—the one with a face that everyone knew about.

Two slashes for eyes and a gaping mouth.

The hungry expression was frozen in the twisted bark, but she could almost feel it watching her, and it gave her the shivers.

Everyone knew the watcher tree rhyme. It had grown into stories that became legend, and it played through Holly's head like a warning now:

I SLUMBER DEEP
BUT STILL I HEAR
EVERY FOOTSTEP
DRAWING NEAR

MY BRANCHES YAWN
MY ROOTS STRETCH
AND THEN I WAIT
FOR A CHILD TO CATCH

COME LITTLE FEET
FIND MY ROOTS
THEY'LL GOBBLE YOU DOWN
ALL BUT YOUR BOOTS

I SEE YOU NOW
IN THE DARK OF NIGHT
WANDERING LOST
FILLED WITH FRIGHT

YOU CANNOT FLEE
YOU CANNOT HIDE
MY ROOTS STRETCH LONG
FAR AND WIDE

THERE'S NOWHERE TO RUN
DON'T YOU SEE
YOU CANNOT ESCAPE
THE WATCHER TREE

Holly had heard the rhyme and stories all her life. From classmates, church camp leaders. Even Daddy, who spun it as a spooky tale around the campfire one night.

The legend said the roots could snake up out of the ground, wrap around a person's legs, and drag them down into the earth. The person would never be seen again because they became a part of the tree forever.

"Jordan, it's the watcher tree," Holly whispered, taking a few nervous steps back.

The stories said it slept during the day and hunted at night, and if their digging hadn't woken it up, she didn't want their voices to. It would snatch them into the ground.

Jordan stood. "Dad says the watcher tree is something someone made up to keep kids from wandering around the woods at night."

But Jordan didn't sound so sure about that.

Tommy from school said one of the roots reached up and grabbed his foot when he walked by last fall. And then there was the little boy who wandered into the woods at night all those years ago and disappeared. All anyone found was his boot at the base of the tree.

Holly took another step back. "We should open the box somewhere else." Somewhere far, far away.

"Let's go to the fort." Jordan squinted at their surroundings. "I don't wanna be here if those guys come back anyway."

"Okay," Holly said, but she cast the spooky tree another glance as she backed away from it.

They gathered up their mysterious box of treasure and digging tools, then dashed through the woods to their super secret hideout.

Jordan tossed away the pine branches leaning against tree trunks and fallen logs to help conceal the hideout from anyone passing by.

The fort was made of layered cardboard from restaurant shipping boxes, held together by tape and a few knots of rope. The roof drooped from the weight of last night's rain, but it was still standing.

It was barely big enough for the two of them, so whenever Gin tagged along, they ended up sitting on each other in order to squeeze in. Jordan was usually the one who got sat on, because he was bigger than the girls.

Holly pushed aside the towel that hung over the opening and yelped as something skittered out. Jordan jumped so high he almost landed in the nearest tree.

A raccoon raced across the damp leaves and pine needles with a plastic package of Twinkies in his front paws.

"Hey!" Jordan shouted. "Those are ours!"

Holly laughed as the furry thief disappeared behind a tree. "I guess we're not the only ones who like Twinkies."

"They'll eat anything. They're scavengers. They get into the trash cans behind the diner and drag stuff out all the time. Mom hates them 'cause of the mess they make."

"We're scavengers too." Holly held up the dirt-crusted box they had found and grinned before ducking into the fort.

Jordan followed, plopping onto the damp ground beside her. When they made their fort, they forgot to cut out windows, and it was dark inside. Holly might not be afraid of the dark—she wasn't scared of much—but it felt like a dungeon to Jordan. He grabbed the flashlight from his bag and clicked it on.

Holly settled the box on her crossed legs. "Did you know they call flashlights torches in Britain? Dad read about it in an article."

Jordan bounced the beam around the small space. "I think that sounds a lot cooler than flashlight. Like you're about to step into a castle."

"That would be awesome. We should build a moat around our fort and hang a flag. Gin and I could paint it."

"Gin would glue sprinkles to it."

They both laughed at that. Gin was convinced sprinkles were a form of fairy dust, and she would sprinkle them on everything if she could get away with it. She once dusted a turtle with sprinkles to see if he could fly. Thankfully, when his fairy wings failed him, he landed in a pile of hay.

"I could be a knight," Holly said.

"You can't be a knight. You're a girl."

Holly straightened her back, the same way she had when he called her pretty. "So?"

"Girls are always the princess trapped in the tower, and men are the knights riding in to fight the dragon and rescue them."

"I don't like that story, and no bully's locking me up in a tower. Girls can be heroes too." She stared at him with narrowed eyes, silently daring him to disagree.

He had the sense not to. "Okay."

A spider swung down from the ceiling into the beam of light in front of his face, and he sucked in a breath, leaning back.

When he moved to swat it away, Holly grabbed his wrist. "Don't hurt him. He's probably scared too."

Jordan jerked his wrist from her fingers. "Too? I'm not scared."

"You're always scared."

"I can be brave if there's a good reason."

"Like what?"

He leaned farther away from the twitching bundle of legs. "I don't know, but I could be brave if I had to. If it was important."

"I think saving a life is a good reason to be brave, even if it's just a spider." Holly picked up a leaf and held it under the little creature, encouraging him to crawl back up the strand of web.

Jordan stared up at the spider on the ceiling as he thought about that. Holly always made him think about things in a new way, and she made him want to be as brave as she was. If he practiced being brave, like he practiced tossing a football, it might get easier. Maybe then Dad would be proud of him.

Holly resettled the box on her lap and brushed the hair from her face. "What do you think is in it?"

Jordan angled the beam of light toward her lap. "I don't know. Money?"

"That's boring. I think it's something amazing. Like . . . dreams."

He rolled his eyes. "You can't put dreams in a box, Holly."

"Says who?"

"I don't know. *Someone.* Dreams are in your head. They can't come out."

"Yes they can. I dreamed of having a friend other than my sister and . . ." She waved her hands toward him. "Poof."

The start of their friendship had been more of a *whack* than a *poof.* He'd been teasing her about her bright orange pigtails, so she whacked him in the face with the tree branch she'd been pretending was a walking stick.

Even though she broke his nose, Dad made him walk to her house and apologize for teasing her. The next school day, she plopped down at his lonely corner of the lunch table, offered him one of her Swiss rolls, and decided they were going to be friends.

That was three years ago.

Having a friend had been one of his dreams, too, and even though Holly scared him at first, he accepted her offer of friendship. Not many people wanted to hang out with the sheriff's son. If not for Holly and Gin, he would still be sitting alone at lunch, tossing rocks over the playground fence at recess.

"I think it's pirate treasure," Holly said, the contents of the box rattling as she turned it upside down and sideways.

"Why would pirates bury their treasure in Kansas?"

"Maybe they got lost."

"They got really lost then, 'cause there's no ocean near Kansas."

Holly frowned. "What about the specific ocean?"

"*Pa*cific, and it's really far away."

"Oh."

Holly loved reading, but she still wasn't very book smart. She was always getting in trouble for daydreaming during class instead of paying attention to history and geography. Ms. Carter, their teacher, told her she needed focus if she was ever going to learn anything useful in life.

But Jordan didn't mind that Holly didn't understand everything he did. She was fun, she liked spending time with him, and she never made him feel like he wasn't good enough.

"I think you should open it." She took his flashlight and passed him the box.

"Why me?"

"Because it'll make you happy."

Holly was always trying to cheer him up when he had a bad day. This morning hadn't started out so well with Dad, but it was getting better.

Excited to see what was inside the box, Jordan tried to pop open the lid, but it didn't move. He tugged at the latch with no luck, then ran his fingers all around the seam, trying to find a lock. There was nothing that should be keeping it shut.

He frowned. "It's stuck."

"Here, try this." Holly handed him a stick.

Jordan stared at it doubtfully. A stick wasn't going to be stronger than metal. But he tried to wiggle the sharp end into the seam. The stick snapped.

"It could be crusted shut, like the ketchup bottle in the fridge," Holly said. "We could use one of the garden shovels to open it."

"Not crusted shut. *Rusted* shut," Jordan said, realizing what she meant. That was what the orangey-looking stuff was on the outside of the box. It was all over his hands now.

19

He grabbed one of the spades from his bag, set the box on the ground, and tried to wiggle the sharp tip of the tool into position, but it was too thick.

He sat up with a sigh. "It won't work."

"Oma probably has something that can open it, and I'm ready for cookies anyway. Come on." Holly snagged the box and crawled out of the fort.

Jordan zipped up his backpack and shifted onto his knees to follow, but the spider swung back down in front of his face. He almost swatted it without thinking, but caught himself.

Saving a life is brave.

Grabbing a leaf from the ground, he nudged the spider back up the silky string to its web on the ceiling the way Holly had.

"Don't jump on my head when I crawl out," he told it, and then he scrambled out of the fort after his best friend.

Stony Brooke was a small town surrounded by farms, fields, and trees. Everything important was in the center—the school, the bookstore, the diner. Oma's Inn was only one street over from Main Street.

The three-story mansion with a wraparound porch sat on a corner. It was painted in several shades of pink, with lace curtains hanging in every window.

The colors were too girly, in Jordan's opinion—blue would be better—but this place was his home away from home. Oma never made him feel like he was in the way or unimportant. Even if she did usually put him to work cleaning or pulling weeds from the flower bed, it was better than being alone.

A rocking chair creaked on the porch as Jordan and Holly climbed the steps, and they found a man gliding back and forth in one of the wooden chairs.

His feathery gray hair was windblown from the storm rolling in, and his jaw was speckled with dark hair.

"Hi, Mr. Potter," Jordan said.

The man dragged his tear-filled eyes from something in the distance, sadness pulling at his lined face. He stared in their direction blankly, almost as if they weren't there, before lifting his empty mug in greeting. "Hello."

Jordan stepped forward. "Do you want some more coffee? I can get you some."

Oma made sure every guest knew they were welcome to the kitchen, but some people who stayed here were so heartbroken it seemed hard for them to breathe. Getting up to refill their own drink wasn't something they thought about. Jordan hoped he would never have to feel that sad.

Mr. Potter blinked into his mug, as if surprised by its emptiness. "I suppose . . . I would appreciate a refill."

Jordan took the mug from him and followed Holly into the Inn. The grandfather clock in the front room donged the hour as they made their way to the kitchen.

*Why was it called a grand*father *clock and not a grand*mother *clock?* Jordan wondered. *Would that make all the littler, newer clocks grand*child *clocks?*

Holly set the treasure box on the oval table that had been squeezed into the center of the small kitchen. "Why do you think that man was crying?"

The heavy coffee pot wobbled as Jordan lifted it from the burner and tipped it to refill the mug. "Oma said his daughter died, and he's here for the funeral and to pack up her stuff."

Holly's eyes widened. "Died?"

"Yeah."

Holly had never lost any members of her small family, so it was hard for her to understand. It had been hard for him, too, before Aunt Mae died. He always liked Aunt Mae and the silly way she turned normal things into songs. She'd been a real-life musical.

"We should give him marshmallow hot chocolate instead of coffee. That always makes me feel better," Holly said.

"He's an old person, Holly. They like boring stuff like coffee and plain bagels. They don't like marshmallows *or* hot chocolate."

"Well, when I'm an old person, I'll still like them." She quirked her lips to one side in thought and then reached for the jar on the counter. "We should give him a cookie."

"You gotta wash your hands before you touch the cookies."

"Oh." Holly studied her dirt-caked nails, then climbed onto the step stool Oma kept tucked under the kitchen table for little guests. Jordan was big enough now that he only needed it for the upper cabinets, but Holly and Gin were small for their age. They needed it for everything.

When Holly rinsed her hands and turned the faucet off, Jordan sighed. "You gotta use soap if you're gonna touch someone else's food."

Holly scowled and then turned the faucet back on.

She didn't know much about being clean around food, but Jordan spent a lot of time in kitchens. At the diner with his mom and here with Oma. He even had his own apron with his name on it.

"Do you think that man will be sad forever?" Holly asked.

"I don't know."

She dried her hands on a towel by the sink and then grabbed a plate and cookie. "Maybe he just needs some cheer." She untwisted the tie on the bag of marshmallows and placed one marshmallow on top of the cookie.

"He's not gonna want the marshmallow, Holly."

"You don't know that."

They filed out of the kitchen, and Holly opened the door for him before following him out onto the porch.

"Here's your coffee, Mr. Potter," Jordan said, holding it out to the man handle-first, even though the mug was hot against his fingers.

The old man drew in a surprised breath and looked at them, as though he hadn't heard their voices or the tap of the wooden screen door as it closed behind them. "Oh, that's . . ." He blinked wet eyelashes as he took the mug. "Thank you."

He set the coffee on the side table and settled back into silence. Jordan tried to think of something to say to make him feel better, but he didn't know what would help.

Holly hopped into the rocking chair next to Mr. Potter, feet sticking off the end, and held the plate out to him. "Marshmallows make me feel better when I'm sad. You should try one."

The older man's eyebrows pressed closer together. "Is that right?"

She nodded. "Chocolate helps, too, but marshmallows are the best." She nudged the plate toward him.

He took the marshmallow and popped it into his mouth, chewing. "You're right, that does help."

"The cookie's for you too."

"And what is the cookie supposed to help with?"

"Making your tongue taste better after you drink coffee, which smells really bad. I don't understand why grown-ups drink it."

Mr. Potter smiled for the first time since Jordan met him two days ago. "My daughter thought the same thing, but then she discovered cappuccinos."

Holly tilted her head, curious. "Cup-a-Cheetos? I like Cheetos."

Mr. Potter's smile made the corners of his eyes crinkle like bird feet. "No, not a cup of Cheetos. *Cappuccinos*. It's a type of coffee." He picked up the chocolate chip cookie. "What's your name, young lady?"

"Holly."

"I appreciate you being a friend to me this afternoon, Holly. You've made this miserable day a little brighter."

Jordan folded his arms and scowled. Holly was *his* friend, not Mr. Potter's, and he thought about telling the man so, but the phone on the kitchen wall began to ring.

By the third ring, he realized Oma must be busy or too far away to hear it. Glancing at Holly and Mr. Potter one last time, he went inside to answer it. Oma didn't mind, as long as he took good notes so she could call the person back.

Oma rounded the corner and shuffled into the kitchen before he could reach the phone. A cobweb stuck to the gray and brown hair on top of her head, waving with her movements. She must've been in the storm cellar out back. That meant really bad weather was coming.

The ringing cut off, and Oma's warm voice announced, "Rosie's Inn." A pause. "Oh, hi, Emily."

Mrs. Emily Cross was Holly and Gin's mom. She was probably wondering if Holly ended up here after running out of the house.

"I haven't seen her, but I've been in the cellar preparing for the storm. Let me check." Oma stepped into the hall, the crinkly phone cord wrapping around her arm like a snake. She smiled at Jordan and then looked past him to the front door.

Mr. Potter's and Holly's voices drifted through the screen. Oma turned back into the kitchen.

"She's here, trying to cheer up one of my guests. That sweet girl can't stand to see a person sad, can she?" Another pause. "No, I don't mind at all. Bring Ginevieve over. We'll make dinner together this evening, and the kids can play games in the den. I'll see you when you get here." Oma hung up the phone and stepped out of the kitchen, offering Jordan a warm smile. "How are you, my sweet boy?"

Jordan looked down at his feet. "Okay."

"I think we should try that again, with a truthful answer this time. How are you?"

Oma never let him skate by with "fine" or "okay." He looked up. "Not too good, I guess. Mom's at work 'cause Saturday evenings at the diner are usually busy, Dad said I would be in the way if I tried to help him build the shed, and Holly's on the porch making new friends."

Oma's face softened. "And you're feeling left out and overlooked."

"I guess so."

"I know your father can be a difficult man, liebling, but he loves you, even if he's not good at showing it. And Holly is comforting a hurting man who will be returning to Florida in three days. You're not being replaced."

Jordan wrapped his arms around her apron-covered waist and hugged her. She always knew the words to say to make him feel better.

The screen door opened, and Holly bounced in like she was crossing invisible hopscotch squares. Her eyes widened, and she grinned before dashing forward and throwing one arm around Oma's waist and the other around Jordan.

Oma laughed. "Now *this* is a hug. It's only missing *one* of my precious little ones."

Holly released her and stepped back. "Gin's at home with Mom, playing dress-up for pictures."

"So naturally, you ran off to play in the dirt."

"I don't like taking pictures."

"That may be, but those pictures aren't for you, liebling. They're for the people who love you. As we get older, we start to forget things, but that one picture, a moment frozen in time, can bring it all back. If your mom wants pictures of her children to help her remember what time tries to make her forget, you let her have them."

Holly squinted as she thought about that. "I guess I can do that. But not in a dress. I don't like dresses."

"You work that out with your momma. I need a picture of all three of you kids for my hallway wall. I have the perfect spot," Oma said, pointing to an open patch of wall surrounded by frames. The entire top half of the hallway was covered in pictures, some black and white, some sort of yellowish, and some colored. They went back generations. "But we'll save that for another day when everyone is here and clean. For now, the two of you need to wash up. I can't send either of you home looking like pups that rolled in the mud."

Oma pulled an old white pillowcase from the closet with three holes cut in the fabric and handed it to Holly.

"You go to the bathroom and put this on so I can wash that dress. Your momma's got enough to deal with without having to do laundry tonight."

Holly took the familiar pillowcase—it wasn't the first time she'd come here covered in mud—and then dashed up the steps to change.

"You know where your spare clothes are, Jordy. Go clean up and put your muddy clothes in the machine." Oma kissed the top of Jordan's head and sent him up the steps.

Jordan squinted, trying to predict his opponent's next move. Would she attack or negotiate for the treasure he held captive?

Holly's bare feet danced on top of the coffee table, and she jabbed at the air with her closed pink-and-purple umbrella, the pillowcase she wore making her look like a shipwreck victim.

"Hand over the treasure, pirate!"

Jordan met her pretend sword with his own, blades smacking together in a fierce battle. "You'll have to take it from me. If you can."

He jumped on the nearby couch with the treasure box tucked in the crook of one arm. Holly sprang onto the opposite side of the couch, slicing at him even as she wobbled. "It's the bottom of the ocean for you, scallywaggle!"

He was too slow to stop her last jab, and she caught him in the ribs. He groaned and dropped his sword into the invisible waves below. He was a goner. The depths would claim him.

Jordan swayed on the soft couch cushion, and the sealed box in his arms slipped free and crashed to the floor with a thud that made both of them cringe.

The rough landing knocked the lid loose, and the contents spilled onto the floor. With a gasp, Jordan and Holly looked at each other and then the treasure.

"Are you two all right in there?" Oma asked from the kitchen.

"Fine!" They called back at the same time, and then scrambled off the couch to inspect the box's secret contents. It wasn't gold, dreams, or even baseball cards. It was a pile of strange and unexpected things.

When Jordan reached for an item, Holly blocked his hand. "Wait! Buried treasure is almost always cursed. We should be careful."

Jordan snatched his hand back. "Cursed?"

What did that mean? Would his fingers fall off if he touched something? Would he be doomed to walk the earth for all eternity like a ghost?

Holly grinned in that way she did when she was teasing him, and he rolled his eyes. He'd fallen for it. Like always. This wasn't even real treasure, and it wasn't buried by pirates, so it couldn't be cursed. It was a box of odd things someone stashed out in the woods.

But why?

Jordan might bury something bad to keep it hidden. Maybe even something important to keep it safe from burglars, but he wouldn't bury the kind of stuff people found squished in the cracks of car seats.

Holly scooped up a harmonica and turned it over in her hands. "This is one of those music things, isn't it?"

"Yeah, a harmonica."

"Do you think it's magic?"

"Why would it be magic?"

"Someone thought it was special enough to hide in a box and bury by the watcher tree where no one else would ever find it. Except we did, so I guess that plan didn't work too well."

"There's no such thing as magic, Holly."

Holly pressed the harmonica to her lips and blew into it. It made a terrible sound—like the trumpeting of an angry herd of elephants—and the lights overhead flickered.

Holly froze with her lips still pressed to the harmonica, her wide eyes sweeping back and forth across the ceiling. Jordan's eyes did the same, but the lights had gone back to normal.

"Play it again," he said.

Holly filled her cheeks with air and blew it into the harmonica, making a noise so loud and awful that it hurt Jordan's ears. The lanterns framing the doorway dimmed and brightened. So did the lamp on the side table.

There was a faint buzzing and then *pop*! The lamp went out.

Holly dropped the harmonica on the carpet. "Maybe we shouldn't play with that."

Jordan wanted to know how it had made the lights flicker—it didn't make sense—but he wasn't willing to touch it and find out. It could break something more than a lightbulb.

"Kids," Oma said from the doorway, and they both jumped in surprise. "The wind is getting stronger, and the power is starting to flicker. If it goes out, I want you to grab the candles from the cupboard under the stairs and make sure every guest has one in their room."

Ha! It wasn't the harmonica. Jordan knew there was no such thing as magic.

"Jordy, did you hear me?" Oma asked.

"Yes, ma'am. Give candles to the guests if the power goes out."

Oma nodded and left them to their investigating.

Jordan picked up a roll of paper tied with a piece of string and opened it. The paper felt crispier and heavier than normal paper, and the ink was faded. He stared at the cursive handwriting, but he still couldn't make out the words.

He held it in front of Holly. "Can you read that?"

She pressed her face close to the paper and squinted. "I don't think that's English. It could be a code or something."

"I wonder if we can figure it out."

"I don't know how."

Jordan made a thoughtful noise and set the cryptic note aside to check out the other stuff. He pushed aside a rock-hard Tootsie roll, a long, gold bullet, and a marble before picking up a roughly carved wooden bear. "This is kind of cool."

"Ooh, pretty." Holly took the bear from him. "I wonder who buried this stuff." She upended the bear in her hands. "There's a name and date on the bottom. Look!"

It was hard to read the numbers and letters scratched into the wood, but it looked like "John, 1918."

"I wonder who John is," Holly said, "1918 is forever ago. Do you think he's older than Oma?"

"Dad says Oma's older than dirt."

"She can't be older than dirt. In Sunday school, Ms. Tawny said we came from dirt."

"I didn't come from dirt. I came from a hospital." His mom and dad had a whole picture album of him when he was a wrinkly raisin wrapped in a blue blanket. And he wasn't dirty like someone who crawled out of the ground.

"There's John from school, but he's not old enough." Holly stared at the carpet in thought. "Maybe it's a Bible verse. There's a John in the Bible."

"Let's check." Jordan hopped up and grabbed Opa's worn leather Bible from the bookshelf. He died of a heart attack when Jordan was only four, so Jordan didn't really remember him, but Oma read from this Bible sometimes. He handed the Bible to Holly. "Here."

Holly set the Bible on the floor between them and opened it. She ran her finger down the table of contents page. "John. Found him." She flipped to that section of the book. "Chapter 19, verse 18. 'Where they . . .'" She paused before the next word and tried to sound it out. "C-r-u . . ."

"It's—"

"Don't tell me. I can figure it out."

Jordan pinched his lips and waited. They had both heard the word in church enough times to know what it meant—Jesus gave His life to save all mankind—but Jordan only knew it by sight because he sat with Oma some evenings when she read her Bible.

"Cruci . . . oh! Crucified," Holly said. "That's how that's spelled. 'When they crucified him, and two others with him, on either side one, and Jesus in the . . . mid . . . st. Midst.' I'm not sure that's a real word."

"It means 'in the middle,' I think."

"Maybe they didn't have enough room to write middle, so they sort of squashed it into a different word. There are a lot of words and not a lot of space."

"It's only one more letter. People back then just talked funny." Jordan flicked the stale Tootsie roll. "It doesn't make sense to put that on the bear. I don't think it's a Bible thing."

"Hmm." Holly closed the Bible. "Oma probably knows who John is. We could find him and give his stuff back. And if we can't find him, we keep it."

Figuring out the mystery of who this box belonged to sounded like a lot more fun than keeping the stuff that was in it. What would they do with a stale Tootsie roll and an old harmonica?

A knock came from the front room, and a moment later, Gin's voice—so much like Holly's, except more childlike—drifted through the house.

"Hi, Oma! Mom says she has to go to work, and I can't stay home alone 'cause I get into things, and she doesn't wanna have to come home and clean the house after a long day 'cause I made a mess. Can I please have a giant cookie?" Gin asked, rattling off the entire sentence without a breath.

"Of course you can, precious," Oma said. "You know where the jar is."

Holly abandoned the contents of the treasure chest and dashed down the hall to see her mom and sister.

Jordan hopped up and followed her into the entryway. Ms. Emily was the tallest woman Jordan had ever seen, but aside from that, she looked like Holly and Gin—pale skin, carrot-red hair, warm brown eyes.

"You're wearing the pillowcase again, I see," Ms. Emily said when she saw Holly's skinny arms and legs sticking out of the fabric.

"This is my uniform for catching thieving pirates. Not a pillowcase, Mom," Holly informed her.

"Her dress is in the washing machine," Oma explained. "I couldn't send it home filthy."

Ms. Emily offered Holly a frustrated look even as she said, "Thank you, Rose. I can never make up for all your kindness."

"You don't have to make up for acts of love, dear. They're freely given."

Holly straightened her pillowcase dress and lifted her chin. "I'm ready for pictures, Mom."

Ms. Emily's eyebrows lifted. "Not in that you're not."

"I mean for next time. I don't want you to forget me, and if pictures help old people remember, I'll sit still for one."

"Old people, huh?" Ms. Emily bent down to Holly's level, hands on her knees. "I have one gray hair. Only one. And it's from you." She tapped the tip of Holly's nose with a finger, and Holly scrunched it in response.

"I didn't make your hair gray."

"Oh, yes you did." Ms. Emily straightened and spread her arms. "Jordan, where's my hug?"

Jordan rushed forward into her arms. He loved Ms. Emily. She was like a second mom, and she always made him feel welcome and loved at her house. "Can

Holly hang out with me a little longer? I don't want her to go home yet."

Ms. Emily gave him a squeeze before releasing him. "That's up to your Oma. I have an emergency surgery. A cat attacked by a wild animal." She turned her attention to Oma. "Cris is doing inventory at the bookstore. I can drop the girls off with him if you're busy or—"

"Absolutely not. I have all my precious ones under one roof for the next few hours. I couldn't be happier."

"Thank you." Ms. Emily closed her fingers around her jingling keys and fixed a hard gaze on Holly. "Behave yourself, young lady, and don't bother the guests."

"I won't."

Jordan grinned and whispered, "Won't behave or won't bother the guests?"

Holly flashed a mischievous smile in reply. She was always getting into trouble for something, and she usually dragged him into it with her.

The screen door tapped shut as Ms. Emily left, and Gin bounced into the room in a frilly dress and sparkling shoes, half-eaten cookie in hand.

"Holly!" She tackled her sister onto the steps with a hug, as if it had been days rather than hours since they last saw each other. She pounced on Jordan next, squeezing him around the neck. "Hi, Jordan."

He patted her back. "Hi, Gin."

Oma smoothed her hands over her patched apron, one of the pockets sagging on one side from loose threads. Jordan had watched her fix it a number of times, and she would break out the needle and thread again tonight. "You kids wash up and set the table for dinner."

"What are we having?" Jordan asked.

"Chicken and au gratin potatoes."

Gin gasped. "Rotten potatoes?"

"*Au gratin* potatoes, my little Ginevieve. I would never serve my precious ones anything rotten," Oma corrected.

"Can we have French fries instead?" Holly asked.

"That depends. How badly do you want homemade French fries?"

Jordan raised a hand. "Bad enough that I'll sweep the porch."

"I'll help peel potatoes," Holly offered.

"I'll, um . . . I can . . ." Gin twisted her dress around her fingers in confusion. "What should I do?"

Oma rested a hand on her head. "You can wash the potatoes for me. Scrub them real good to get all the dirt off."

Gin popped onto her toes with excitement the same way Holly always did. "Okay!"

The three of them followed Oma into the kitchen to clean and prepare dinner.

Jordan swept the porch with the straw broom, but the stormy winds blew the dirt back onto the porch. He scowled at a leaf he couldn't seem to get rid of. He even tried throwing it once, and it flew back and smacked him in the face.

He slapped it down with the broom bristles before it could skip away, and snatched it up, stuffing it into his pocket.

I win, he thought. There was no way it was escaping from his pocket. He swept the rest of the dirt back into a pile, but before he could sweep it off the porch, Gin twirled through it.

"Gin!" he shouted.

She never paid attention to what she was doing, and she made things so much harder.

"Gin-Gin," Holly said. "Jordan's trying to sweep, and you need to stay out of the way."

"Oh. Sorry, Jordan," Gin said.

He sighed. "It's okay."

He couldn't stay mad at her. She couldn't pay attention to everything because her brain worked differently. Oma said he was supposed to love her for the unique way God made her, and he did. Usually.

Gin kissed his cheek, giggled, and twirled away. Yuck. Jordan wiped his sleeve across his cheek. Kisses were gross.

"I think my peeler's broken," Holly said, giving the butchered potato in her hand the evil eye. Each swipe of the blade flaked off a speck of skin and left a gouge in the white of the potato.

"It's not broken. I use it all the time," Jordan told her. "You're just doing it wrong."

Holly glared at him. "Am not."

"Yeah, you are. You're messing it all up, and it's not even that hard to do."

"Jordy," Oma said in that warning tone she used when he'd done something wrong. "There was a time when you didn't know how to do it either, but I taught you. Instead of criticizing how she's doing it, offer to show her how _you_ do it."

"Sorry, Holly," Jordan mumbled.

Oma offered her peeler and potato. "Well, go on then. Show her how I taught you."

Holly lifted her chin. "I can do it myself."

41

"It's okay to admit when you don't know how to do something, Holly. All that means is you have an opportunity to learn something new. And it's important to always be learning."

Jordan leaned the broom he was sweeping with against the railing and came over, taking the potato and peeler. He sat down beside Holly. "Don't press too hard. It's gotta be soft, long strokes. Like this." He showed her, and she tried to mimic his method.

Her lips puckered to one side in concentration as she dragged the blade across the skin. By the third attempt, she managed a long strip of brown peel, and she brightened with her accomplishment.

Jordan grinned. "You got it."

"You see? Helping someone learn and succeed feels better than tearing them down, doesn't it?" Oma asked.

Jordan nodded as he passed the dinner items back to her. "Yeah, it does."

"And learning something new is worth the effort, isn't it, my expert potato peeler?" she asked, and Holly nodded.

Gin snatched up the long potato peel, held it above her upper lip, marched across the porch, and said in a deeper voice, "I'm Officer Mustache, and I'm here to collect all your Skittles! Hand 'em over."

Oma pressed a hand to her chest. "Demanding all my Skittles without just cause ... that sounds like robbery."

"No, no. I'm not a robber. There's ... um ... there's a cause. It's be*cause* I like Skittles."

Jordan leaned toward her and whispered, "You need them because they're evidence, Officer Mustache. Dad says evidence is important."

Gin puffed out her chest. "I need them 'cause I'm an officer, and they're epidence."

Jordan slapped a palm to his forehead at the way she said *evidence* wrong. Typical Gin.

"Oh, well, in that case, I might be able to hand over a few after we clean up the dinner dishes. But only a few, Officer, since I know for a fact you already had a cookie," Oma said, and Gin hopped up and down with excitement.

Jordan kicked his chair into motion, the rusty springs squeaking. "Oma, do you know anyone named John?"

"I know quite a few Johns."

"This one would be really old."

"Anyone over twenty seems old to you kids. You'll need to be more specific."

"Like 1918 old."

"Hmm," Oma said in thought. "I knew a John when I was a girl. He was quite a bit older than me,

43

probably ninety or so now. But he moved away some forty years ago."

Great. How were they going to find this John if Oma didn't even know him? She knew *everyone* in town.

"Does this have something to do with that box you two were messing with in the den?" Oma asked.

"We found it in the woods, and we wanted to give it back to whoever it belongs to," Jordan explained.

"You're right about it belonging to someone older. It's an ammunition box from World War I. Whoever this John is, his father probably served in the war."

Jordan frowned. Dad mentioned the world wars sometimes and something about Germany, where Oma's parents had grown up. "Was the war really bad?"

"All wars are bad, liebling. Sometimes they're waged for good reasons, like saving the innocent and taking down evil leaders, but there's an unimaginable cost of life. And sometimes the soldiers come home brokenhearted because of all they've had to see and do on the battlefield."

"That's sad. I don't like war," Gin said. "I like fields of flowers better than fields of battle. We should plant flowers everywhere, and then everyone would be happy and nice."

Oma smiled. "Life would be much better if people were kind and loving to each other the way Jesus said we should be."

Holly paused in her peeling. "What about bullies? Do we have to love bullies? Because they're mean jerks, and I don't like them at all."

Oma shifted toward her in her rocking chair. "Is someone bullying you?"

Holly shrugged a shoulder in answer.

Oma made a thoughtful noise. "We love them because God loves them, but we don't like how they behave or the choices they make. And most people are mean because they're hurting deep inside and don't know how to deal with that hurt. The mean things they say to you usually aren't even about you, even if it feels like they are."

"So we have to let them pick on us?"

"Never. You should tell a grown-up. No one has the right to bully you, and if they're picking on you, they're not getting the help they need for *their* pain either."

Holly looked at Jordan, but he shook his head. He didn't want to talk about the boys from the woods. He wanted to forget about them, and the best way to do that was to focus on the treasure.

"Do you know how we can find John?" he asked.

"You can check the local phone book for Johns in town," she suggested. When they both jumped up, she said, "*After* dinner and cleanup."

Holly and Jordan groaned and resettled in their chairs. They would need to eat and do their chores quickly so they could solve the mystery.

45

The storm crashed into the town after dinner, rain pattering against the windows like hundreds of tiny feet running across the glass.

Gusts of wind rattled the shutters and knocked out the power on the street. Holly watched the neighborhood houses go dark at the same time as theirs. The lights in the windows puffed out like blown birthday candles.

Holly didn't mind the darkness, but Gin's wail of fear had stretched through the whole house. Oma distracted her by letting her help dry dishes. One slippery plate had already hit the floor and shattered. It was a good thing Oma had lots of dishes.

After passing out candles and matches to the guests upstairs, Holly and Jordan returned to the den and built a tent, draping sheets over couch cushions and dining room chairs. They huddled around the treasure box, Jordan with a flashlight and Holly with a bowl of miniature marshmallows for dessert.

"John Berkshire's address isn't too far from the church. We could walk there after," Jordan suggested. "Berkshire first, and then . . ."

The French doors behind them rattled, and they both fell quiet. Was that the storm? The doors rattled again.

Holly crept out of the tent and peeked around the side at the glass doors. A bolt of lightning brightened the back porch, and a figure with two short legs and tree branches sticking every which way stood outside.

She gasped and nearly choked on the marshmallow that had been smoothed against the inside of her cheek.

A tree with arms and legs.

The legend was true. The watcher tree could send out a part of itself to hunt—a sapling watcher. It walked around almost like a person, except it was made of roots, limbs, and vines.

"What is it?" Jordan crawled out the other side in time to see the figure disappear down the steps. "What was wrong with his arms?"

"It's the watcher."

Jordan's face said he didn't want to believe, but how could he pretend it wasn't true? Even the grown-ups knew it was true.

"The legend says you can't escape the watcher tree once it sees you. There's nowhere you can go that its roots can't find you. We took the box from him, and he saw us," Holly explained.

Jordan swallowed hard. "Mmm, maybe it's John. Dad said he arrested a guy once who attacked someone because they touched his stuff. What if John knows we dug up his box and he wants it back? That makes more sense, doesn't it?"

"You saw his arms. They were branches."

"I . . . I don't know. That could be what I saw. It's dark, and he was already walking away."

Holly scowled at him but didn't argue. There was an ancient and dangerous monster outside, and this wasn't the time to argue. "What if he's mad and trying to get inside?"

Jordan's eyes widened. "Oma never locks the front door."

He scooped up the treasure box and his flashlight and darted for the front door, Holly's bare feet pattering down the hall behind him. They raced past the kitchen into the foyer and nearly crashed into the screen door.

The watcher sapling clomped up the steps onto the porch. He was coming straight for them.

"The door, Jordan!" Holly shouted.

Jordan slammed the interior door and bolted it. He leaned back against it, breathing hard, the treasure box clutched to his chest. "He can't get in now."

Heavy pounding made Holly suck in a breath, and she threw her weight against the door too. The creature's clobbering fists vibrated the wood against their backs, and they looked at each other, unsure what to do.

Could the watcher pound his way through the door? Would the hinges and locks be strong enough to stop him?

"If we toss the box out a window, do you think he'll take it and leave?" Holly asked.

"We can't open a window. He'll climb through it and come after us."

The pounding stopped, and the porch boards creaked as the watcher sapling stomped around outside. Was he looking for another way in? Were all the windows locked?

A floorboard *inside* the Inn groaned, sending their hearts tripping in their chests, and Jordan snapped his flashlight toward the hallway.

Oma raised a hand to shield her eyes from the beam of light. "What in the world is going on out here? I heard pounding. And why are you two standing in front of the door?"

"There's a monster outside," Holly said.

"A monster?" Oma asked as she approached.

"The watcher. The evil tree with the face that gobbles up people. We saw his sapling with its tree branch arms and everything, and it's trying to get in."

Oma blinked a few times, like she was struggling to process Holly's explanation, then said, "Trees aren't good or evil, liebling. They're only trees. Now, come away from the door, both of you."

"But—" Jordan began.

"If there is someone out there who needs shelter from this storm, we're going to let them in, even if they do have tree stumps for arms."

Branches, Holly thought. *Not stumps. Wasn't she even listening?*

"Away from the door," Oma instructed. "Don't make me ask a third time, or I'll put both of you in time-out in separate rooms until your parents come pick you up."

Jordan hung his head and then shuffled away from the door. Holly hesitated—she needed to protect Jordan and Gin—but then obeyed. What choice did she have?

Oma unlocked the door.

Holly stood beside Jordan and straightened her back, leaned onto her toes, and lifted her chin, making herself as big as possible. She would make the watcher think twice about hurting her friend and sister.

Oma opened the door and then propped open the screen. "Hello?" she called into the storm, and her voice brought the stomping footsteps back.

The creature stepped inside, rain dripping from his raincoat onto the doormat. Wait . . . trees didn't need to wear raincoats. And where had his tree branches gone? He wasn't made of twisted roots and twigs like Holly expected.

A man's voice came from the dripping hood of the raincoat. "Sorry about the mud on my boots, Rose."

Hold on a minute. Holly knew that voice.

He flipped back his hood, revealing his face.

Holly lowered her fists and let her heels drop back to the floor. "Daddy?"

Her dad stood on the welcome mat in a gray raincoat, smiling at them. "Hey, Jelly Bean."

Holly squinted past him into the night. "Did you see a tree out there?"

"I saw a lot of trees out there."

"No, one that was moving."

His forehead wrinkled. "It's storming, honey. There isn't a still tree in town."

Holly huffed in frustration. He wasn't understanding what she was saying. "A live, moving tree monster, Daddy."

"Ohhh," he said, drawing out the word as he crouched in front of her. "Has someone been telling you stories about the watcher tree again?"

"They're not just stories. He's real, and he sent his sapling after us. It has tree branches for arms and everything."

"I know I told you kids about the watcher tree during one of our backyard camping nights, but remember I said it was only a legend. One that's been around for more than a century. It can't come after you or anyone else."

"But then what was outside?"

"What you saw out back was me picking up fallen branches from the steps so no one would trip and fall."

Holly frowned. "Why were you back there?"

"Rose asked me to pick up some new batteries and Gatorade for emergencies. I put them in the storm cellar and thought I would come in the back to escape the rain. It was locked, so I came around front, but someone closed the door in my face." He looked up at Jordan, who ducked his head apologetically. "I guess now I understand why."

"So . . . there's no monster outside?"

"Nope. It was only me." He tapped the tip of her nose with an affectionate finger and then stood. "Mom's running a little behind, so I'm here to take everyone home. Jordan, I can drop you off at your house so your parents don't need to come out in this."

"Thanks, Mr. Cris."

"I'll grab Holly's dress from the laundry room," Oma said.

Gin trotted in, spotted Daddy, and rushed forward with a squeal. "Daddy!"

He scooped her up in a hug. "You ready to go home, Gingersnap?"

"Yeah." She held out a hand and opened her fingers. "Look what I got! Four quarters for helping with dishes. I can buy candies at the store!"

"Yes you can." He nuzzled her nose with his, and she giggled. He looked down at Holly. "Time to go, Jelly Bean. It's almost your bedtime."

"We have to go put away our tent." Holly grabbed Jordan's arm and dragged him back down the hall to the den. Together, they took apart their tent and put everything away. "Do you wanna keep the box tonight and bring it to church tomorrow? I think it'll be safe with your dad in the house. No watcher or bogeyman John will come after it."

Jordan rubbed his lips between his teeth, trying to decide. "Yeah, I guess that'll be okay. And I kind of wanna show my dad anyway. It's pretty cool. Maybe he'll think so too."

Holly picked up the last pillow and tossed it on the couch. With the den all clean and tidy, they headed back to the entryway.

"Goodnight, Oma." Holly wrapped her arms around the old woman's waist and hugged her.

"Goodnight, liebling," Oma said, then kissed each of the kids on the head and nudged them out the door.

Holly and Jordan paused at the edge of the porch to watch the storm, and Holly's lips spread into a grin. "Race you to the car."

"Bet you get wetter than I do."

They bounded down the steps into the stormy night, trying to outrun the raindrops to the car.

Mr. Cris dropped Jordan off in the driveway of his family's home, and Jordan found the front door unlocked. He went inside, the treasure box tucked beneath one arm.

Candles sat around the living room. The power must've gone out here too. Hopefully it wouldn't be down for too long.

Dad's calm voice came from the kitchen. "I guarantee you he was with those twins all day again, doing something pointless like planting flowers or playing make-believe."

Jordan looked down at the dirt-crusted box he'd been holding while playing pirates with Holly, and for the first time since they dug it up, he felt ashamed.

"There is nothing wrong with a ten-year-old boy playing make-believe, and those girls are his friends," Mom said. "They love him, and he loves them."

"I've got nothing against the Cross family, but he should be making friends with boys his age, not playing pretend with little girls. He needs to learn how to be a man."

Jordan's shoulders slumped under the familiar criticism, and his eyes burned with tears.

"He's ten, Jed, not sixteen, and he won't learn how to be a man from other little boys. That's something he should learn from his father. If you spent more time with him—"

"I don't know what to do with him, Tammy. He doesn't like fishing or hunting, he's got no backbone, and he can't tell a wrench from a screwdriver," Dad said, every shortcoming he listed making Jordan shrink even more.

"*Teach him.* You can't expect him to automatically know what you know and be interested in things he doesn't know how to do. And you could try meeting him on his level," Mom replied.

"Is that some New Agey parenting technique you read in a magazine?"

"Try some of the things that interest him."

"I don't do little girl tea parties."

"Jed—"

"I'm tired from working on the shed by myself all day. I don't want to talk about this anymore tonight." His footsteps thumped across the kitchen floor toward the living room.

Jordan slipped soundlessly back outside into the darkness, closing the door behind him. As he walked through the backyard, pain and anger swirled into a violent storm in his chest—more violent than the storm whipping the trees around him.

He threw the treasure box to the ground, grabbed the miniature shovel from his backpack, and plunged it into the edge of the flower bed. Hot tears mixed with the rain on his face and dripped from his chin as he stabbed and tore at the dirt.

Stupid buried treasure. Useless pretend games. He didn't want anything to do with either of them anymore. He was a man, not a little boy.

He wiped a dirty hand across his face to erase the tears and then shoved the box into the hole. He piled dirt over it with both hands and packed it down.

The evidence of his childishness was gone.

He sat back on his knees, lower lip quivering with emotion, and then threw the shovel across the yard. It thumped against the side of the new shed—the shed he wanted to help Dad build this morning, but he didn't know enough to be anything more than in the way.

Surging to his feet, he grabbed a fallen tree branch and stormed the shed like it was a castle he needed to smash apart stone by stone. He slammed the branch against it over and over, attacking from all sides as he yelled out his frustration.

He would never be good enough for his dad. *Whack!* Never know enough. *Slam!* Never be man enough. *Crack!* Why was he never enough?

"Jordan!" Mom's voice was like a bucket of ice water over his anger, and he staggered on the last swing. She stood in the back doorway, barely visible in the dim glow of candles burning on the kitchen counters behind her. "What are you doing?"

Jordan's chest heaved as he gulped in air and fought back tears. He looked down at the branch he held as the reality of what he'd done crashed into him. The shed was covered in dents and scratches, and the window was cracked.

He turned back toward the house to find Dad stalking toward him. Jordan stiffened. He was in trouble now. He flinched when Dad ripped the branch from his hands and pinned him with a look of disappointment rather than anger.

"This is something overly emotional little boys do. Learn how to control yourself, or you'll never get anywhere in life."

Fresh tears pooled in Jordan's eyes.

"Go clean up and go to your room. I don't want to see you for the rest of the night," Dad said, and stepped aside to let him by.

"You don't wanna see me *ever!*"

Jordan slipped past Mom in the doorway and ran to his room. He slammed the door behind him and collapsed on his bed. He had too many feelings right now, and he didn't know what to do with them, so he buried his face in his pillows and screamed.

Holly stared out her bedroom window at the trees twisting and snapping in the storm. Deep in the middle of those dark woods was a winding road, and on the other side, about a fifteen-minute walk, was Jordan's house. Their home was outside town, so the Radcliffe family was their closest neighbor.

She hugged her stuffed bunny to her stomach and ran her fingers over its ears, worried.

Daddy said the watcher tree was only a legend, but she was certain he was real. As certain as she was that the sun would come up in the morning. All her life, she'd heard stories about the watcher tree—from grown-ups *and* kids. Not *everyone* could be wrong.

She shouldn't have told Jordan to take the treasure box home with him. What if he was in danger now?

She sucked her bottom lip between her teeth in thought. She could slip on her rain boots and coat without waking anyone and run to his house to check on him. She knew the way even in the dark.

Yes, she would run over and check on him, then run back and hop in bed before anyone even noticed she was gone. She slid her feet off the bed and grabbed one of her polka dot rain boots.

Lightning zigzagged through the clouds, brightening everything for a second, and then thunder crashed so loudly Holly could feel it rumble through the walls of the house and into her chest.

"Holly." Gin's whimper came from her bed on the other side of the nightstand. "I'm scared."

Holly glanced at the window one more time, her plan dissolving like marshmallows in hot chocolate. She couldn't leave Gin alone and scared.

"It's okay, Gin-Gin." She set her boot back on the floor. "I'm coming. Scooch over."

Another long bolt of lightning brightened the room, and Holly used it to see as she scampered across the toy-cluttered floor. She dove beneath the blanket Gin held up.

When her knee hit something hard, she felt under the blanket and realized Gin was holding her piggy bank. "Why is Penny in the bed?"

"She's scared," Gin whispered. "We have to keep her safe from the storm."

Holly twisted so she could watch the window. It was closed and locked, but sometimes the curtains moved like something was breathing behind them. There was nothing there. Only air seeping in through the window, Daddy said.

A tick against the outside of the glass made both of them jump, and Gin curled closer to Holly's back, her toes like little ice cubes against Holly's legs. "Is it a monster? Don't let it get us."

"I won't."

"You promise?"

"I promise. I won't let any monsters get you."

She would battle a fire-breathing dragon to protect her sister, even if it did turn her into an extra crispy chicken nugget with one flaming sneeze.

A dark shape crashed into the window. The girls screamed and ducked beneath the covers to hide from whatever was trying to bust into their room.

Footsteps thumped down the hall, and the bedroom door flew open, light pouring in. Holly poked her head above the covers to see Daddy in the doorway with a flashlight.

"What happened? Are you girls okay?"

Holly pointed to the window. "Something smashed into it." And she bet she knew what, but she couldn't say it out loud with him beside her.

Daddy walked to the window and looked out. Mom wrapped her robe around herself as she came in after him, dodging toys in her slippers.

She looked over his shoulder. "What is it?"

"Part of the dead limb snapped off the tree and hit the window."

Mom pressed her hand to her chest. "Hard enough to crack the glass? If the wind were any stronger, it could've broken through and hurt the girls. Holly's bed is right there, Cris."

"I know."

"I asked you to take care of that limb weeks ago."

Daddy sighed. "I know, Em. I forgot, and I'm sorry. I'll take care of it tomorrow evening."

Holly slipped from the bed and padded over to the window to peer out. She couldn't see much of anything, so she looked up at Daddy. "Are you sure it was a dead tree limb? Not something scarier?" She lowered her voice to a whisper so Gin couldn't hear. "Like a monster?"

Daddy scooped her up and propped her on his hip. He pressed his flashlight to the glass so the light shone through it. "Look there. See that old limb where your tire swing used to be?"

"Yeah, it's broken."

"Look down there." He tipped the flashlight so she could see the ground. There was a long, dark shape lying in the grass. "Nothing scary." He carried her back to Gin's bed and set her on the edge of it before crouching down. "You girls have nothing to worry about. I'll keep you safe."

"Penny and me are too scared to sleep," Gin admitted, hugging Penny the piggy bank tighter. "Can we have story time and cookie snacks?"

Mom knelt beside Daddy and smiled. "It's too late for cookies, and you need sleep, not stories. We have church in the morning."

"But I *can't* sleep," Gin cried.

"What do we do when we're scared?" Mom asked.

Gin rubbed wet cheeks on her sleeve and whimpered, "I don't remember."

"Yes you do."

Holly leaned in close and whispered, "We say a prayer."

Gin sniffled and announced, "We say a prayer."

Daddy smiled at Holly—he'd seen her whisper the answer to Gin—and then offered his hand.

Once their hands were all connected, Mom said, "Pray it with me, girls. Jesus sir, I come to thee."

"And ask you please watch over me," Holly added, then looked at Gin for her part.

"Keep me safe. Dry my tears."

"Protect me from the things I fear," Daddy finished, and together they all said, "Amen." He kissed both of them on the top of the head. "Good night. I love you."

He tucked them in side by side, placed Penny safely on the nightstand, and then he and Mom left the room.

"Holly is asking about monsters?" Mom whispered in the hallway.

"The watcher tree," Daddy said.

"I told you they're too little for your spooky campfire stories."

"They enjoy them."

"Our daughter is worried about being eaten by a monstrous tree, Cris. No more campfire stories." Mom's and Daddy's voices faded as they walked down the hall to their bedroom.

Holly cuddled close to Gin as the door closed, feeling safe and warm after Daddy's promise of protection and family prayer. No monster or storm could get them tonight.

Sunday school, Jordan thought with a scowl. He would rather count the rocks in the gravel driveway this morning than sit on the floor of this hot classroom with kids who ate their boogers and peeled the paper off crayons while the teacher read them a story.

Today's lesson was about Moses and the plagues of Egypt. Like Jordan cared about some old guy with a long beard and a stick.

All he wanted to do was leave. He could take his baseball cards to the fort in the woods and hang out by himself for a while. If he was alone, no one could make him feel bad for not being good enough. And it would be cooler than this classroom.

Without power, there were no fans and no air conditioning, and if he didn't get out of this room soon, he might melt like an ice cream cone. Ms. Tawny would have to mop him up with paper towels, and it would probably take a whole roll.

"And then . . ." Ms. Tawny leaned forward in her chair, meeting each of their eyes. "The frogs came. Imagine them hopping everywhere. Underfoot, in the drinking water, in your beds."

A collective giggle and *ewww* from the little kids made Jordan roll his eyes. Frogs weren't scary or gross.

One of the boys raised his hand. "Why did God send frogs?"

"Good question, Brian," Ms. Tawny said. "No one can know God's exact reasoning, but one possible explanation is . . ."

Jordan tuned out Ms. Tawny's voice as he stared out the open classroom window. It wouldn't be so hot if there was a breeze, but the storm last night seemed to blow away all the wind. It was as still as roadkill outside.

Maybe he could ask to use the restroom and then sneak out for the morning. But if he did that, Oma would be disappointed in him too. She was the one who made him come this morning.

Gathering in God's house is good for the soul, she'd said.

But Mom and Dad never came. Mom was always too busy preparing for the lunch crowd at the diner, and Dad didn't care for church. If they weren't here, he shouldn't have to be either.

Gin, who sat beside him, poked his knee with a finger and held up a blue crayon that had snapped in two and was barely clinging together by the wrapper. "Can you fix my crayon?"

"No one can fix it. It's broken."

"But I don't want it to be broken."

"You pushed too hard. That's what happens."

Gin pouted and tried to fix the crayon herself, but she couldn't keep the pieces together.

Holly leaned over him from the other side and handed Gin a strip of tape. "Wrap it around the break like a Band-Aid," she whispered, then looked up at Jordan. "What's the matter?"

"Nothing."

"You're sad."

"No I'm not."

"Yes you are. It's in your eyes."

"Be quiet. You're gonna get us in trouble."

Holly shifted her jaw sideways in annoyance. She didn't like it when he told her to be quiet, but she was always getting them in trouble for talking when they were supposed to be quiet. "Do you still wanna go find out who the treasure box belongs to after church?"

"I'm a man now. I don't play stupid, pointless pretend games with little kids." It felt good to let out his anger and hurt, but the good feeling only lasted until he saw the tears in Holly's eyes.

She shot to her feet and out of the room. Jordan started to get up and go after her, to say he was sorry, but Ms. Tawny's voice stopped him.

"Stay seated until class is over, Jordan."

"But I need to—"

"You all are my responsibility for the hour, and I don't want you wandering in every direction. Heather." When Ms. Tawny said the name, a teenage girl looked up. "Go see if you can find Holly."

The girl left the room.

Jordan fisted his hands in his lap. He wanted to find Holly himself. She was *his* friend. Ms. Tawny went back to reading the book in her lap.

Gin looked up at Jordan with wide, confused eyes. "You made Holly sad. Why?"

The question made Jordan feel as low and icky as a slug, and he wanted to find a rock to hide under. "I didn't mean to." He wished he could take back the words he'd said to Holly.

When the classroom door opened, he expected to see his best friend coming back, but it was only Heather. He frowned at the empty hallway behind her.

Heather crouched beside Gin. "Your mom wants to see you." She offered a hand. "Grab your stuff and come with me."

Gin hopped up, took her hand, and left with her without question. Jordan had questions—where was Holly, why was Gin leaving early, and why couldn't *he* leave early? He raised his hand to ask if he could.

Ms. Tawny paused in her reading. "Jordan, if your question isn't about the story, it can wait until after class."

Jordan bit back a groan of frustration and dropped his hand. He tapped his knees in rhythm with the clock on the wall, waiting for class to be over. Why was it taking so long? Could time actually slow down?

"That's all for today, kids," Ms. Tawny finally said. "You can color until your parents come get you."

Jordan wasn't sitting around waiting for Oma to come get him like he was four. He knew how to get to the sanctuary on his own without getting lost. The church wasn't *that* big.

He rushed out of the room, dodging adults who stood in the hallway talking. He spotted Oma in the sanctuary, but the seats beside her where Mr. Cris and Ms. Emily usually sat were already empty.

"Excuse me," he said, pushing his way through the church crowd to the parking lot. He searched for the familiar purple station wagon Holly's parents drove, but it was gone. "No, no, no."

Jordan kicked at the fat gray stones of the parking lot. They had already left.

Someone slammed into him and knocked him forward. "Out of my way, Rat-cliffe."

Jordan shrank away from Mike, who was so mean it was a wonder he didn't bounce off an invisible barrier when he tried to enter the church. He obviously didn't learn anything about being kind from the preaching.

"Where's your little girlfriend?" Mike taunted, shoving Jordan and making him stumble again. "She finally ditch you?"

Jordan rubbed at the spot where Mike's hand had connected. He wanted to say something smart back, but the giant fifth grader would squash him like a bug and then smoosh him into bug paste with his shoe.

"Mike!" a woman called out from the parking lot—probably his mother. "I need to get ready for my shift at the hospital. Let's get going. You can talk to your friend later."

Friend? Was she blind?

"Catch you some other time, rat boy." Mike left him standing alone at the edge of the parking lot.

Jordan kicked at another chunky gray stone in anger. He wanted to pick them up and hurl them at Mike's back, but then Mike would do more than shove him around. Today was the worst day ever.

"There you are," Oma said, coming up behind him. She rested a hand on his shoulder. "I saw you talking to Mike. Are you two—"

"We're not friends!" Jordan balled his fingers into fists. "He's a bully, and I hate him."

"We never hate people, Jordy. What we hate are the bad things they do and how they make us feel, remember?"

"Fine. I hate how he calls me names and pushes me around just 'cause his dad got himself arrested on Christmas. That's not my fault. His dad did something wrong. Not me."

69

"You're right. That's not your fault. I'll talk to his mother."

Jordan folded his arms and grumbled, "I don't care about him."

"Then why are you so upset?" Oma asked.

"I said something mean to Holly 'cause I was mad, and she left. The whole family did. I didn't even get to say sorry. She's gonna hate me now."

"Oh, now you know that isn't true. Holly has the biggest heart of anyone you've ever met, and she doesn't hate anyone."

"She ditched me like Mike said."

"She was upset, so they decided to leave a little early and go to the bookstore. She didn't *ditch* you. If you tell her you're sorry, she'll forgive you."

Jordan swiped at a tear sneaking out of his eye. "You think so?"

"I *know* so." She ran a hand over his hair. "Why don't you come back to the Inn with me. We'll eat the last of the ice cream before it melts."

He thought about it for a second, then shook his head. He needed to go home and dig up the box he buried. He wanted to impress his dad and make him proud by being a man, but he didn't want it to cost him the only two friends he had.

The front window of Criss Cross Books was dark, and the open sign was off, but Mr. Cris's car was parked by the curb.

The picture window was covered in construction paper flowers in a rainbow of colors. Jordan and the girls had cut and glued them together last week because Mr. Cris wanted to add a little touch of spring to the shop.

Jordan tucked the treasure box under one arm and opened the door, setting off the jingling bell overhead.

"I'll be right with you," Mr. Cris called from somewhere between the packed shelves of books.

The girls weren't in the kids' section on the bench with the fountain in the center, so they must be in the back in one of the big chairs. Jordan usually headed straight back to join them, but he wasn't sure he was welcome today.

Their laughter drifted through the bookstore, and he felt a pinch of sadness that he wasn't a part of it. He needed to make things right with his friends. Somehow.

Mr. Cris appeared with a few books in his hands and paused when he saw Jordan standing by the door. He set the books on a cart with a stack of others. "Jordan, is everything all right?"

Jordan fidgeted with the treasure box. "I . . . um . . . I wanted to talk to Holly. To say sorry to her for . . . what I said at church."

Mr. Cris fixed the glasses slipping down his nose, the ones he only wore when he was reading. "I appreciate that you want to apologize for hurting her feelings."

"Would it be all right if I go back?"

"I think you and I should talk first."

Jordan hung his head—he didn't want to hear about how bad of a friend he was—and mumbled, "Okay."

"Come help me shelve these books."

Jordan set the treasure box behind the register and followed Mr. Cris and the cart of books down one of the aisles. "I know I made Holly cry, and I'm really sorry about that."

"I know you are. We all make mistakes, especially when we're upset, and we all need a little grace."

"What do you mean *grace*?"

"Instead of getting angry about the mistake you made and wanting to get you back for it, I can be understanding and offer you forgiveness. Like God does with us." Mr. Cris handed him a book. "Would you shelve that on the bottom for me? My back's feeling a little stiff."

Jordan bent down and slid the book into an open space. "So you're not mad at me for making Holly cry?"

"No, I'm not mad. When someone is hurt, that's usually when they say hurtful things to other people. You want to tell me what drove you to say those things to Holly?"

Jordan tapped his toes against the bottom of the bookshelf. "Dad and Mom were talking last night, and Dad said I should be more of a man than a boy, and I shouldn't be playing make-believe with little girls."

Mr. Cris was quiet for a moment before he said, "I see. And what do you think being a man means?"

"I guess . . . like my dad. But I don't wanna lose my friends and say things that hurt people."

Dad didn't have any friends. He had his work and his family, and he didn't need anyone else. But Jordan did. He wasn't happy sitting on a creek bank by himself with a fishing pole or out in the woods alone with a rifle. He needed friends to spend time with.

"There are a lot of ideas out there about what makes a man a man," Mr. Cris said.

"Which one's right?"

"There are all kinds of men in the world. Good men, bad men, men somewhere in between. I can tell you what I think makes a *good* man, but my opinion will be different than your dad's."

"I wanna hear it."

Mr. Cris added a book to a higher shelf. "A good man cares about people and considers what's best for everyone instead of always thinking about himself and his wants. A man who only thinks about *his* wants and needs is selfish."

Jordan chewed on that, trying to figure out if he was selfish. He didn't think so.

"He's willing to listen and learn instead of believing he knows everything," Mr. Cris continued. "A good man is willing to admit when he's wrong and do what he can to make things right."

Jordan could admit he didn't know everything, and he was here to say he was sorry for doing something wrong.

"He leads with kindness and respect. He uses his strength to protect people smaller and weaker than him. He never uses it to hurt them," Mr. Cris added.

"Holly and Gin are smaller than me, but Holly's definitely stronger than me," Jordan admitted. She could wallop him if she wanted to.

Mr. Cris smiled. "That won't always be the case."

Jordan thought about all the information Mr. Cris had given him. His dad fit a couple of things on the list, but not all of them. "Does that mean my dad *isn't* a good man?"

Mr. Cris paused in thought. "Do you know what character is?"

"It's all the stuff that adds together and makes us who we are. Our character," he said confidently. Oma had explained that to him before.

"Yes. All the things I just told you about are pieces of a good man's character. Pieces, not the whole picture. Your dad has some good pieces to his character, but he's imperfect like everyone else."

"I don't know." Jordan picked at the corner of an old sticker one of the girls had stuck on the edge of a shelf. "You seem like the perfect dad. Sometimes I wish you were my dad too."

Mr. Cris crouched beside him. "I'm not a perfect man or a perfect dad. You know that tree outside the girls' bedroom window?" When Jordan nodded, he explained, "Emily asked me to cut down some of those limbs weeks ago, but I didn't listen. Last night, one of the dead limbs broke off and cracked the girls' window. They could've gotten hurt because of my mistake. Perfection has only walked this earth one time, and His name is Jesus. No one else will ever come close, and if we expect them to, we'll be disappointed. We all make mistakes. What's important is that we learn and grow."

Jordan chewed on that. "I wanna grow. I wanna be better."

Mr. Cris rested a hand on Jordan's shoulder and looked at him in a way his dad never had—like he was proud of him. "My little girls are blessed to have a friend like you."

The compliment made Jordan feel a foot taller. "Really?"

"Really. You keep growing, and you will be an amazing man one day. But for now, be an amazing boy." Mr. Cris nodded toward the back of the shop. "The girls are in the comfy chairs."

"Thanks." Jordan started toward the register to grab the treasure box, then stopped. "Mr. Cris, please don't tell my dad what I said about wishing you were my dad instead."

"That stays between you and me."

"Thanks. Can I help cut down the tree branches so the girls don't get hurt?"

"Come by the house this evening, and we'll work on it. And anytime you want to help me around this shop, my back would appreciate it. I am an old man, after all."

Jordan grinned. "Yes, sir." Unlike his dad, Mr. Cris liked his company *and* his help, and that felt good. He dashed back to grab the treasure box and then headed for his friends.

Holly and Gin were squeezed into an oversized striped chair together, feet sticking off the end, while Holly read from *The Wizard of Oz*.

"But I don't like tornadoes," Gin broke in. "They're scary. What if our house gets sucked away next?"

"It won't," Holly said, sounding sure. "Besides, Daddy said tornadoes are just God sneezing, remember?"

"Yeah, I . . . I remember, and . . . we should get God some medicine like Daddy takes so . . . um . . . so he doesn't have allergic sneezes. They break a lot of stuff."

"Good idea."

Holly had stopped believing tornadoes were from God's sneezes years ago, but the story their dad told them helped Gin feel less afraid when the skies turned dark and the wind picked up.

"Holly, what do we say to God when He sneezes?" Gin asked, tilting her head to one side. "God bless . . . yourself?"

"Hmm. That's a good question. I bet Daddy knows the answer. He knows all kinds of stuff."

Jordan stepped forward. "Um, hi."

Holly closed the book and studied him, looking as prickly as the thistles he'd pulled from Oma's flower bed last week. "You shouldn't be here with us little kids."

Jordan flinched.

"Yeah, that was a mean thing to say, Jordan," Gin said, then glanced at Holly and whispered, "I think I forgot. Are we still mad?"

Jordan moved forward another step. "I'm sorry for what I said. I take it back."

Holly narrowed her eyes, trying to decide whether or not to accept his apology, and then nodded once. "Okay. I forgive you."

Jordan sagged in relief. Oma had been right.

Gin sat up straight. "Are we friends again? I like it better when we're friends."

"Yeah, we're friends," Holly said.

"Yay!" Gin cheered. "I wanna show Jordan my princess dress." She wiggled out of the chair, stumbling on her clear plastic slippers, and twirled in her sparkly blue costume dress. "Don't you love it?"

"Um . . ." Jordan readjusted the heavy box in his arms. "It's very pretty, Gin."

Unlike Holly, Gin was a girlie girl, and she enjoyed being told she was pretty. She practically glowed at his compliment.

"I'm gonna wear it when I get married, and everyone's gonna throw sprinkles. Daddy . . ." Gin wandered off between the bookshelves. "Can I have sprinkles at my wedding?"

"I brought the t-r-e-a-s-u-r-e box so we can find out who it belongs to," Jordan said. He didn't want to say the word treasure out loud because Gin might overhear and want to come, and she would slow them down by sniffing every flower and petting every stray cat.

Holly closed the *Wizard of Oz* book and scooted from the chair. "Let's do it." She grabbed Jordan's free hand and took off, dragging him down the aisle toward the front door. She shouted good-bye to her dad and Gin and then burst out onto the sidewalk.

"Do you think Gin will be sad we left her behind?" Jordan asked, glancing back at the bookstore.

Gin was very attached to Holly, and she wanted to be with her all the time, but Gin couldn't do everything they did, so sometimes they had to sneak away and leave her behind.

"Daddy will make her some marshmallow hot chocolate and read her a princess story," Holly said. "She likes *Snow White and the Seven Dwarfs*. She says the little people are cute."

Jordan opened the glass door to Mom's diner. "Let's get some snacks. I'm starving."

He waited for Holly to go in first. He'd seen Mr. Cris open doors for his wife and the girls. He said it was how a gentleman treats a lady. Not that Jordan would *ever* call Holly a lady to her face. She would knock his eyes crooked with a tree branch.

The diner was dark except for the glow of a few candles, and the booths and tables were empty. Without power, Mom couldn't prepare any food for the Sunday lunch crowd.

"Mom?" Jordan called out, his voice echoing in the unusual emptiness.

"I'm in the kitchen, baby," Mom called back.

Jordan walked between the tables and back into the kitchen, where Mom was doing inventory for the restaurant. He leaned against her and scanned the list she was working on. "Did we lose anything from the power outage?"

"Not yet. These coolers and freezers will hold their temperature for a while, but I drove to the neighboring town to get extra ice just in case." She wrapped an arm around him. "How was church?"

"I don't wanna talk about it," he grumbled.

"That bad, huh?"

"Sort of."

"Any plans with the twins today?" Mom asked.

"Yeah, but we're hungry. Is there anything we can have for lunch?"

"I want to avoid opening the cooler, but how about some peanut butter and jelly sandwiches and a cookie for dessert?"

"A cookie *and* marshmallows," he negotiated.

"Those marshmallows wouldn't happen to be for a certain little redhead blowing out the candles in my dining room, would they?" Mom asked, picking up the scent of candle smoke in the air.

"Yeah, they're her favorite."

Jordan didn't mind marshmallows, but he preferred cookies or ice cream. He grabbed the peanut butter and jelly from the stockroom shelf while Mom opened a loaf of bread. He set them on the food prep counter in front of her.

"I'm sorry about the shed, that I broke the window and stuff." He hadn't said he was sorry last night because he was too mad to mean it.

"I know you are, honey, but you need to learn to think about the consequences *before* you act. It's never okay to destroy other people's things, and your dad worked hard on that shed."

"I didn't mean to get so mad, but . . . I did, and I didn't know what to do. My whole body felt like it was gonna explode."

Mom wrapped an arm around him and gave him a squeeze. "Emotions are big things, and sometimes they're hard to deal with. But we'll figure it out as a family, okay?"

"Okay. Do you think Dad would mind if I tried to fix the shed?"

Mom hesitated to answer. "I'll talk to him about it when I bring him lunch."

"If he asks what I'm doing today, please don't tell him I'm spending the day with Holly. She's my friend, and

81

I wanna hang out with her, but I don't want him to be disappointed in me again."

Mom's butter knife stilled in the peanut butter. "Did you hear our conversation in the kitchen last night? Is that why you got so upset?"

Jordan stared at the floor as he nodded.

Mom crouched in front of him, tears sparkling in her eyes. "Sweetheart, listen to me. Your dad has strong opinions, things he learned from his dad, but just because someone's opinion is strong doesn't mean it's always right. There is nothing wrong with you spending time with your friends. Nothing whatsoever. Holly and Gin are good, kind girls, and I know how happy they make you. I want you to have fun adventuring today, and don't worry about what your dad said last night."

"Okay."

"But be home for dinner at seven."

"Would it be okay if I ate dinner with Holly's family tonight instead? Mr. Cris said he could use my help to trim one of his trees after, and I really wanna help."

Mom smiled, but there were still tears in her eyes. "Sure, baby. I think it would be a good idea for you to spend some quality time with Mr. Cris. And I'm sure he'll appreciate having a strong young man to give him a hand."

Jordan lifted his chin proudly. "That's what I was thinking."

"Be home before nightfall. I don't like you being alone in those woods after dark."

Jordan didn't like being alone in the woods after dark either. He didn't believe in silly legends like man-eating trees or anything like that, but there were coyotes and the occasional wolf, and they might eat him.

Mom finished the sandwiches and filled a plastic bag with marshmallows, handing them to him. "You two have fun and be careful. And Jordan . . ." She lowered her voice. "Don't do anything you know you shouldn't, even if Holly thinks it's okay. She doesn't always understand when something's a bad idea, so you need to speak up."

Holly did have some not-so-great ideas sometimes, and he had to explain things to her. Today would probably be one of those days.

"I'll be smart, Mom, don't worry."

She kissed his forehead. "I know you will."

"Love you." He hurried into the dining room with their lunch. Holly was breathing in smoke from one of the blown-out candles when he stopped beside her. "Sandwiches."

"Oh, yum!" She took hers. "Don't you think candles smell like birthday cake when you blow them out? I love it."

They did sort of remind him of birthdays. He grabbed Mom's lighter from behind the counter and relit them, brightening the room. "Come on, we can eat on the way to Mr. Berkshire's house."

Holly stepped over a raggedy boot lying in the road as they made their way to the first house on the list. The mate was in the grass with broken flowers and dirt spilling out. They must've blown off a porch and tumbled through the grass during the storm.

It hadn't been a tornado last night, but with the downed branches, knocked-out power, and people's stuff everywhere, it made almost as much of a mess.

Holly ate a few miniature marshmallows from the plastic baggy and then offered some to Jordan. He grabbed some and tossed them into the air, catching two of the four with his mouth.

"Why can't I ever do that?" Holly asked. If she even came close to catching the marshmallow, it was with her eyeball or the side of her nose.

"You have terrible aim."

"Do not."

"Do too. Remember the last time we were playing catch, and you tried to toss the football back to me?"

Oh yeah . . .

She missed him completely and broke the wind chime Mom had dangling from the porch roof. She would have to practice more, especially with the marshmallows, because that would be a cool trick.

She looked at the piece of paper with addresses in her hand and then at the lopsided mailbox in front of them. One of the numbers was missing, but this had to be the right place. "We're here."

Jordan fidgeted beside her on the road. "It looks spooky. We should skip this one."

Holly took in details with narrowed eyes. It did sort of look spooky with the porch swing hanging from one chain, and the grass tall enough to be a jungle. But it looked more sad than anything—like the two windows upstairs with droopy drapes were the eyes, and the open door downstairs was the crying mouth.

"I don't believe in ghosts or anything, but that place has to have something creepy living in it. Giant rats, most likely," Jordan said.

"Don't worry. I'll keep you safe."

Jordan shot her a scowl. "I'm bigger than you. Maybe I'll keep *you* safe."

Holly doubted that, but she only said, "Okay."

She dragged open the squeaky wooden gate attached to the fence that surrounded the yard, and started up the sidewalk. Jordan groaned and followed.

Holly hopped up the slanted steps onto the porch and peeked through the open doorway into the dark house. "Mr. Berkshire, are you home?"

Jordan peered past her. "It sure is dirty in there. Do you think he ever cleans?"

"No, and the dust bunnies could be holding him hostage." She leaned forward, the tips of her shoes brushing the entryway floor, and strained to see more without going inside. "Mr. Berkshire, I think we found your treasure box. Is it okay if we come in?"

No one answered.

It couldn't hurt to go in and look around. He could be too tired to get out of bed. Or his hips went wobbly and he fell down. Mom said it happened to old dogs, which meant it probably happened to old people too. He could be hurt.

Holly stepped inside, but Jordan grabbed her arm and tugged her back onto the porch with a frightened whisper. "You can't go inside, Holly."

"Why not? The door's open."

"'Cause he could be a bad person."

"There's no bad people in Stony Brooke."

"That's not what Dad said, and he's almost always got someone locked up in the jail," Jordan explained. "Good people don't usually go to jail."

Holly had never really thought about that. Except for some mean bullies, she'd never met a bad person in Stony Brooke. There might be bad people in other towns, but not here.

"Can we at least check around back first before we disobey my dad's rule of don't-go-in-a-stranger's-house?" Jordan asked.

"Sure."

Holly led the way around the wraparound porch, dodging junk piles and sticky spiderwebs, but she went as still as a statue when a dog rounded the far corner.

He was as big as she was—head low, pointy teeth bared—and a deep, rumbling growl came from his throat. Holly's heart skipped in her chest, and she inched back, bumping into Jordan.

"I guess checking the backyard was a bad idea," Jordan said, his voice shaking. "What do we do?"

Holly tried to remember what Mom had told her about aggressive dogs. She was a vet; she knew how to deal with all kinds of animals. "Don't run."

"*Don't* run? If we stay here, he's gonna use us for chew toys."

"Mom says sometimes they chase you if you run." Jordan might get away, but she had short legs, and she wouldn't make it out of the yard.

The dog stepped forward, drool dripping from its mouth, and they yelped, stumbling back into a pile of junk.

Holly dropped the bag of marshmallows and grabbed up a broken chunk of the porch railing, gripping it like a bat as they inched backward. "Bad dog. Stay back."

He snapped his teeth, and Holly flinched. She didn't want to get eaten by a dog today. Or any day.

Jordan kept one hand on Holly's shoulder and the other wrapped around the treasure box as they slunk backward. "What's wrong with him?"

"He could have rabies. Mom says that happens sometimes." And if he had rabies, there would be no calming him down and patting his head. No apologetic puppy kisses. He would tear into them like they were crispy drumsticks and coleslaw.

"We need help," Jordan said.

"You should go find a grown-up. I'll . . . I'll scare him with this so he doesn't follow you." She waved the chunk of railing.

"Leave you alone?"

"I don't know what else to do, Jordan." She didn't *want* him to leave her, but she didn't want them *both* to get eaten by a dog. Gin would need him if something happened to her.

"We can try to distract him." Jordan picked up a stick and tossed it, but the dog didn't even notice it as it landed in front of his paws.

Holly swallowed. They were done for.

"Rubio! Settle!" a man bellowed, and the dog snapped its mouth shut on one final growl, then sat down, looking as polite and gentle as a teddy bear.

Holly and Jordan whirled toward the man who had shouted. He stood on the porch behind them. He was a toothpick of a man, and his silver beard hung down to the middle of his belly. His big toe poked through a hole in one of his boots.

"Rubio doesn't like people on our property," he said, his huge hand gripping the handle of an axe. "Neither do I."

"We're sorry. We'll go now." Jordan snatched Holly's hand and tugged her, but she dug in her heels. They had come here for a reason.

"Are you . . . Mr. Berkshire? J-John Berkshire?" she asked, swallowing her fear. Hopefully, he hadn't brought that axe with him to chop them into firewood.

He bent down until his beard brushed the dirty ground and narrowed his eyes. "I know you. You're Emily Cross's little girl. One of those twins she's got pictures of all over."

Holly lowered the chunk of railing in surprise. "You know my mom?"

"She's the only vet in town." He nodded to his dog. "She treated Rubio for an infected bite on his back leg a couple of days ago."

"Oh." Holly glanced back at the dog. She would be in a bad mood, too, if something had chomped on her leg a few days ago. "Is he better?"

"He's getting there." He turned his eyes to Jordan. "And you're the sheriff's son. You ought to know better than to go snooping around other people's property without permission."

Jordan's shoulders drooped.

"We weren't snooping!" Holly objected. She wasn't going to let him make Jordan feel bad for something they weren't even doing. "We called for you because we wanted to talk to you, but you didn't come out.

We were gonna see if you were around back. That's not snooping, so don't say it is when it isn't."

Mr. Berkshire straightened, his forehead folding into half a dozen wrinkles. "My, my. Aren't you a little spitfire."

Holly eyed him sideways as she held on to the chunk of railing. "I don't spit fire. I'm not a dragon. And if I was, I would be purple. But I'm not."

Mr. Berkshire took the chunk of railing from her hands, and she stumbled forward, trying to hold on to it.

"Hey!" she shouted. "That's mine."

"Actually, it's mine. *These*"—he picked up the bag of marshmallows—"puffed cavities are yours." He handed them back to her. "What do you children want?"

Jordan released Holly's hand and hefted up the treasure box. "We found this in the woods yesterday, and it belongs to someone named John, but we don't know which John."

"Hmm." Mr. Berkshire studied the box without touching it. "It's not mine. I've never had a box like that. It's awful nice you two are trying to find out who it belongs to instead of keeping it."

"Daddy says we should always do the right thing, even if no one's looking," Holly said.

"Your daddy's a wise man. Must be all those books he reads."

"You know my daddy too?"

"Young lady, there are less than fifteen hundred people in this town, and I've lived here my entire life. I know almost everyone. Except for some of the littler folks."

"Do you know any other Johns this box might belong to?" Jordan asked. "We made a list, but we could've missed someone."

"Let me see what you've got."

Holly passed him the crumpled paper.

He scanned the names, his face drooping into a frown. He plucked the pencil from behind his ear and scratched out one of the names.

"Hey!" Holly popped onto her toes, trying to see whose name he'd scribbled out. "You can't cross them out. We haven't visited them yet."

"And you won't be visiting him." Mr. Berkshire scribbled the name and address out of existence. They would have to look it up in the phone book again. "He's not a good man, and it's not a safe place to go."

"Did he do something illegal?" Jordan asked.

"Yes, and don't ask me what it was because I won't tell you. But you keep away from his house, you hear?" He looked at Jordan. "Promise me you two won't go knocking on his door. Together or alone."

Jordan nodded. "Yes, sir." Then he leaned toward Holly and whispered, "I told you there were bad people in town."

"I don't have anyone else to add to your list," Mr. Berkshire said, handing it back. "Do your parents know what you're up to and where you're going?"

Holly and Jordan shook their heads.

Mr. Berkshire tucked the pencil back behind his ear. "At least *I* know now. Someone should always know where you are and who you're with." He squinted at the sky. "You two better get moving. There's only about four hours of daylight left, and you're a ways from the center of town."

"Thanks," Holly said, letting Jordan tug her toward the front of the porch. She paused at the top of the steps. "Mr. Berkshire, why don't you mow your grass or clean your house?"

Mr. Berkshire frowned. "Don't you think that's a rude question to ask a person?"

"No."

He sighed. "It may have escaped your notice, young lady, but I'm an old man. Old age comes with problems."

"Like your hips?"

"Nothing wrong with my hips. It's my heart. It's old, and it's tired. The doctor said if I do anything strenuous, anything that gets my blood pumping too much, my heart could stop altogether." He looked around at his dirty house and overgrown grass with a hint of sadness. "I do what I can here and there."

"Can't your family help?"

"I'm all that's left of my family. Never did have kids."

Jordan tugged on Holly's arm. "Come on. We gotta go or it's gonna get dark before we're done."

"Go on now," Mr. Berkshire said.

"Bye! Thanks for not letting your dog eat us!" She waved and hopped down the steps beside Jordan.

She took one last look at the messy property before they left. When Mom was sick and couldn't clean, Daddy took care of her and the house. He said love involves taking care of people when they can't take care of themselves. Holly wasn't sure what, but there had to be *something* she could do for old Mr. Berkshire.

"John Lemon," Holly said, looking from the house number to the address on her paper before she stuffed it back into one of her overall pockets.

She frowned at the odd fence in front of them. It didn't enclose the property at all. It was only the gate, and it only blocked the sidewalk. "Where's the rest of the fence?"

"Maybe it fell down?"

"All of it?"

"I don't know." He shrugged and pointed to the sign attached to the fence. "Beware of gnomes."

Holly's face scrunched. "Usually it says dogs. Do you think they have attack gnomes?" She stood on tiptoe and squinted at the yard, searching. She gasped and pointed. "I see one."

Jordan followed her finger to the chubby gnome hiding in the grass, a shovel pointed at them like a spear. "Uh . . . that's a weird-looking gnome."

"He doesn't look happy we're here."

"He's made of clay, Holly. He doesn't have feelings."

"You don't know that. He might come to life at night and guard the yard. There could be a whole army of attack gnomes with feelings," she teased.

"That would be kind of cool, actually."

Holly quirked her lips to one side as she stared at the little gate. "Should we go through it or walk around it?"

"I think we should go over it." He passed the box to her and backed up, bending low. Holly watched him with wide eyes as he launched forward and sprang over the fence, landing in a crouch on the other side. He raised his hands in the air. "Who's the champion?!"

"My turn." Holly set down the box and tried to figure out how to climb over the fence. She lifted a leg to see if she could step over, but she was too short. "I wonder if I can run and jump like you did."

"You're not a good jumper."

"But I'm a good climber. Better than you."

Jordan crossed his arms. "Only 'cause you cheat."

"Do not." She grabbed the top of the fence, stretched onto her toes, and then climbed over. She hopped down beside him with a grin. "Tada!"

"You left the box over there."

"I needed my hands." She stepped around the fence and scooped it off the ground, bringing it back to him.

As they walked up the sidewalk toward the front porch, Holly watched the ground. There were creepy gnomes hiding all over in the grass. They weren't the typical gnomes—cute guys with smiles and mushrooms. They looked grumpy and ready for a fight. Especially the ones lining the porch steps.

"I don't think I like gnomes," Holly whispered, then threw him a scowl. "And not 'cause I'm a fraidy cat. They look mean, and I don't like mean things."

"I didn't say you were scared."

"Good. 'Cause I'm not."

Jordan shifted the box to one arm and knocked on the door. Heavy footsteps approached from the other side, and the door opened a moment later.

The woman who appeared in the opening caught Jordan by surprise. She was toad-like and dressed in a black robe. Her dark hair, with a gray skunk streak, frizzed in every direction as if she'd been zapped by one of the lightning bolts last night.

She wiped her hands on her robe before opening the screen door, and Jordan noticed the red streaks across the fabric. Red . . . like blood. What had she been doing before they knocked on the door?

"My goodness." The old woman leaned down to study them. "Aren't you two the cutest and most unexpected little visitors?" She said in a high-pitched voice. She reached out and pinched Holly's cheek. "I could just eat you up."

Holly's eyes widened, and she stepped away from the woman and closer to Jordan, whispering, "Wicked witch. I've read this story. We should go before she tries to fatten us up and eat us."

"You read too many books," Jordan said.

Holly scowled. "There's no such thing."

"There's no such thing as witches."

"Yes huh. The Bible says witchcraft is bad, so there are too witches. They're as real as you and me. You can ask Daddy. He'll tell you. And look, she even has a witchy broom by the door."

It was the same kind of broom Jordan had swept Oma's porch with last night. There was nothing spooky about that.

"Did you say something, dear?" The old woman cocked her head like a bird. "You'll have to speak up. I don't hear so well these days."

"Do you eat kids?" Holly asked.

"Well, of course I do. Who doesn't eat pigs?" Her eyes drifted to the side in thought. "Vegetarians, I suppose."

Holly and Jordan frowned at each other. Pigs?

The woman opened the door wider. "It's a warm day. Why don't you two come in and I'll fix you a snack and something to drink while we talk about why you're here. Do you prefer cake or cookies? Or we could splurge and have a little of both."

Holly pinched her lips and shook her head at Jordan. He doubted the old woman was a witch, but that didn't mean they should go in her house and eat her food.

When Holly only stared at her distrustfully, Jordan said, "No thanks. We're not hungry."

"What does being *angry* have to do with eating cake and cookies?" the woman asked, then tilted her head again. "Actually, I do eat a lot of chocolate cake when I'm upset. That makes . . . oh. Oh, you said you're not *hungry*, didn't you? I misheard."

"Yes, ma'am."

"Well, that's all right then. Are you two selling something for church camp? Chocolate pastries perhaps?"

"No, ma'am. We wanted to talk to Mr. Lemon."

"I'm Mrs. Lemon."

Jordan spoke louder. "Could we speak to *Mr.* Lemon?"

"Oh, that old toad is gone."

"Gone where?"

"Moved on to a younger woman. No telling where they are now. He took most of our money and the car when he left. I said, 'Why don't you just take the fence, too, since you're taking everything else?' And . . . you can see how that worked out." She waved a hand at the remaining gate. "He took everything except the part that's cemented in the ground."

Jordan wasn't sure what to say to that. He only wanted to ask Mr. Lemon about the box. "Can you call him?"

The woman's hand flew to her chest. "Can I *kill* him? Heavens no. That's a crime. Which isn't to say I haven't considered . . . actually, it was more of a passing thought. I would never truly—"

"What's all over your robe?" Holly asked.

Mrs. Lemon looked down at herself. "This is my painting smock. I'm a bit wild with my acrylic paints, and they go everywhere. I wear this to protect my clothes when I paint my gnomes."

"It's not blood?"

"Blood . . . gracious me. You do ask unusual questions, don't you? What would make you think it's blood?"

"It's really red, you said you could eat us up, *and* you look and dress like the witches from some of the books in Daddy's bookstore," Holly explained, eyeing the woman. "And you have a broom right by your door."

Mrs. Lemon didn't react for a long while, and then she coughed and choked like an old car engine before she started to laugh. "You are an uncomfortably honest child." She patted her chest as the laughter faded. "If that's the image I'm portraying, it must be time to visit the salon.

I know I haven't taken much care with my looks since John left. I rarely leave the house except to get groceries and ship orders."

"Ship orders?" Holly asked.

"You didn't think all these gnomes were for me, did you? People order grumpy gnomes from my website, and I ship them all over the country." She pointed to a sign in her yard that read Tulip's Gnomes.

"Oh. I thought maybe you were building a gnome army to scare people away."

Mrs. Lemon laughed again. "I suppose it does look like an army. I ran out of storage space in my shed, and this is the overflow."

Holly hooked her thumbs into her pockets and rocked onto her toes. "Sorry I thought you were a witch."

"That's all right. Why did you want to speak with my ex-husband?

Jordan explained about the treasure box and opened it to show her the contents. "Do you think it might be his, since his name is John? There was a date on the wooden bear—1918."

Mrs. Lemon tipped her ear toward him. "What was that date?"

"1918," Jordan repeated.

She shook her head. "John is only sixty eight. He wasn't even born in 1918. And these look like things a child would've placed in the box."

Jordan sighed and closed the lid. Another swing and a miss. If they skipped the house Mr. Berkshire told them to skip, they only had one house left. If that one was wrong, too, what would they do then?

"I'm glad you children stopped by. I don't get many visitors these days, and I haven't laughed in a long time," Mrs. Lemon said. "Here, you take these for the road. Fuel for your quest." She pulled two suckers from the pocket of her smock.

"Ooh, cherry." Holly reached for one.

"Dad says we shouldn't take food from strangers," Jordan said.

Holly paused with her fingers inches from the treat. "But it's my favorite flavor."

Mrs. Lemon reached inside the house and grabbed fifty cents. "How about this instead? A quarter for each of you to buy yourselves some suckers at the store. That way, no one gets in trouble."

Holly turned her hand palm-up. "Wow, thanks!"

Jordan thanked her too. He would rather have a gum ball than a sucker. A blue one. He pocketed his quarter. "Thanks for talking with us, Mrs. Lemon."

"Anytime. I appreciate the company."

Jordan squinted at the lowering sun and then at Holly. "We better head back to your house. If we're late for dinner, we'll be in trouble."

"Be careful on your way back to the street. Those gnomes can be feisty, and you never know when they might spring into action and come for your ankles," Mrs. Lemon said. "And if you take the woods, be sure to get home before dark. Some of the trees will be waking up soon, if you know what I mean."

Holly gaped at Jordan, and he mumbled, "She's only kidding." At least he hoped she was kidding.

They tiptoed their way down the sidewalk, past the creepy gnomes, and back out onto the street.

Everyone sat around the fire in the backyard, roasting hot dogs over the flames. If Jordan arrived early enough next time, maybe he could help build the fire. It couldn't be that hard.

"Who wants to hear a campfire story?" Mr. Cris asked. Ms. Emily threw him a warning look, and he cleared his throat before adding, "Something cute about . . . Care Bears perhaps."

Gin threw up her hand. "I love Care Bears!"

"Can we do a spooky story?" Holly asked, her hot dog dipping down into the flames when she looked away from it. Jordan nudged her stick back up with a finger before she could blacken her dinner.

"Um . . ." Mr. Cris glanced at his wife's expression and said, "No spooky stories tonight, Jelly Bean."

"I don't wanna hear about Care Bears."

"I do!" Gin raised her hand higher, trying to make her vote count more. "Rainbow Sprinkle Bear and his adventures in . . . um . . .um . . . cotton candy land."

Jordan swallowed a groan. Baby stories. He would rather hear something cool about adventures or mythical creatures. He rotated his hot dog over a patch of coals. "Mr. Cris, are witches a real thing?"

"That's a good question," Mr. Cris said. "They're not green, they don't wear black robes, and they don't fly around on broomsticks like in the Wizard of Oz." He smiled at Gin and Holly, who had been reading that book earlier today. "But yes, witchcraft is real. There are people who choose to worship spirits of darkness rather than God, and they mess around with rituals and spiritual elements they shouldn't."

Ms. Emily cleared her throat. "The girls, Cris. No more spooky stuff, remember?"

"Right. Why the sudden curiosity?"

"Holly thought Mrs. Lemon might be one, and I might've wondered for a second, but . . . we were wrong," Jordan explained.

"I told her I was sorry," Holly said.

Mr. Cris smiled. "That's my girl."

"Daddy." Holly's hot dog dove back into the flames. Jordan rolled his eyes and nudged her stick back up without a word. "I wanna help Mr. Berkshire."

103

Mr. Cris's eyebrows pinched in thought. "Berkshire. That name sounds familiar, but I can't put a face to it."

"He's an old man with a bad heart. He can't mow his grass or clean anything, and the inside of his house is a mess," Holly explained.

Mr. Cris leaned forward in his chair with concern. "You went in his house?"

"No, she wanted to, but I didn't let her go in," Jordan blurted, explaining before either of them could get in trouble. "We only went on the porch."

Mr. Cris turned to Jordan. "Do you remember what I said about a man protecting others?"

"Yes, sir."

"Good job. I'm proud of you."

Jordan's chest swelled at the praise. Holly had been about to make a bad decision by going into a stranger's house, and he protected her from it.

"Can I go help Mr. Berkshire?" Holly asked. "Please? He doesn't have any family or friends to help him, and no one should have nobody."

"Why don't we go pay him a visit tomorrow evening as a family and see what we can do for him," Ms. Emily suggested. "It's important to help out people in need."

Holly kicked her feet through the air in excitement. "Can I push the mower?"

"What's the rule about the mower?" Mr. Cris asked.

"I can't push it until the bar is at my belly button."

"And where is it now?"

Holly puffed out a disappointed breath and mumbled, "My nose."

"You have a lot of growing to do, Jelly Bean."

Ms. Emily helped the girls put their hot dogs together, and they said grace before digging in. After they were finished, Holly hopped up. "We're gonna play with bubbles. You wanna play, Jordan?"

"No, your dad needs my help trimming the tree," Jordan said proudly. He followed Mr. Cris to the shed.

"Gloves to protect your hands and glasses to protect your eyes." Mr. Cris handed both to Jordan, and he put them on.

He felt like a grown-up in his gear. He couldn't believe Mr. Cris was letting him help with this. Dad would never let him because he might mess something up.

"What if I do something wrong?" he asked.

"If you make a mistake, you learn from it, and that way, you won't make it again. I learned to always wear goggles when working with things that splinter because I nearly blinded myself with a splinter to the eye when I was younger."

Jordan's eyes widened. "Really?"

"Yep. I messed up, I learned from it, and I did better the next time."

"What do you want me to do?"

"I'm going to climb up there and cut off pieces of the dead limb. I need you to help me move them to a pile by the shed. They're heavy, so don't drop them on your toes. And it's important to stay clear until the log is on the ground. That way, you don't get hit."

"Yes, sir."

Mr. Cris stood and held out a hand. "Let's do this, partner."

Jordan grinned and slapped his hand, nearly losing his oversized glove. He watched from the sidelines as Mr. Cris leaned the extended ladder against the side of the house and climbed up with a chain saw.

"Keep the girls back, Em!" Mr. Cris shouted before putting on his protective goggles and bringing the chain saw to life with the jerk of a string.

Jordan watched with excitement as the first chunk of limb plunged to the ground. It landed with a *whomp!* And bits of bark flew everywhere. He looked up at Mr. Cris, who nodded, and he raced forward to pick up the chunk of wood and carry it over to the side of the shed.

Mr. Cris hadn't been joking. The logs were heavy, and by the fourth armload, his muscles were sore. He turned back toward the tree and saw Gin fluttering out of the house chasing bubbles she'd blown from the container in her hand.

She was too close to the tree.

Jordan's heart kicked around in his chest, and he looked up at Mr. Cris, who was focused on the spot the chain saw was chewing through. He scanned the area for Ms. Emily, but she must still be inside from when she took the leftover food in.

"Mr. Cris!" Jordan shouted, but he kept sawing at the limb, unable to hear him. What should he do? Gin could get hurt, and if he rushed over there to get her, *he* could get hurt.

His palms started sweating as he tried to decide.

"Gin! Get away from the tree!" he finally shouted, then darted toward her at the same time Holly did. His legs were faster, and he snatched Gin by the arm and dragged her away as the chunk of limb dropped.

The rotten wood hit the ground not too far from where Gin had been playing and exploded into pieces. Gin dropped her container of bubbles and let out a terrified wail.

Mr. Cris turned off the chain saw and looked down, spotting the three of them. "Gin?" he called out, worried. He started down the ladder. "Emily!"

Ms. Emily sprinted out of the house toward them. "I told her to stay in the living room while I went to the bathroom. I didn't realize she came back out." She scooped Gin up and checked her over. "Are you okay, honey? Are you hurt?"

"The mean tree . . . made me s-spill my bubbles," Gin hiccupped, fat tears rolling down her face.

Holly held out her container. "Here, Gin-Gin, we'll share bubbles. You can have a turn."

Gin sniffled as she took the container. "Thanks, Holly." She smeared her tears with her sleeve. "You're my favorite sister."

"I'm your only sister, Gin-Gin."

Mr. Cris dropped the chain saw on the ground and came to check on Gin, who stretched out her arms so he could take her. He stroked her back, shushing her and telling her the scary moment was over. She was safe. He looked down at Jordan through Gin's tangle of red hair and said, "Thank you for looking out for her."

Jordan wasn't sure what to say. He kicked at a piece of stray bark and mumbled, "She's my friend, and I didn't want her to get hurt." He caught Holly smiling at him and asked, "What?"

"I guess you really can be brave when there's a good reason."

Was this what brave felt like? Jordan's heart was still beating too fast, and he felt shaky all over—like when he missed the last step on a staircase and felt himself falling, only to realize he was safe. He'd saved Gin, but he'd nearly been clobbered by a tree doing it.

Jordan's shoes crunched over sticks and bark as he walked into the woods to head home for the evening. The sun had dropped behind the trees, and the woods were fading into shades of gray.

He glanced behind him to see Holly standing on the invisible line between her family's property and the woods. She'd asked if she could walk him home, but both her parents said no. If she walked Jordan home, she would be walking back in the dark.

She strained forward on her toes and waved good-bye before the path veered to the right and led him out of sight. He was on his own now, and somehow the woods felt spookier than usual.

A slithery breeze rustled the leaves overhead, and one of the branches bobbed as something scurried across it. It had to be a bird. Or a squirrel. Yeah, definitely a squirrel.

A snap from somewhere nearby made Jordan jump, and he stumbled over his own feet as he scanned the gray woods for something big enough to snap a twig.

"H-hello?" he called out. "Is someone out there?" He fumbled the flashlight from his backpack and clicked it on, casting the beam left and right.

Nothing but nature.

"Holly?"

Maybe she didn't listen to her mom and dad and snuck out to walk him home anyway.

Another snap and shuffle. Someone—or some*thing*—was definitely in the woods with him. A shadowy figure moved in the corner of his vision, and he sucked in a breath.

The old woman's warning popped into his head: *Be sure to get home before dark. Some of the trees will be waking up soon.*

"I don't believe. I don't believe in the watcher tree. It's not real," Jordan muttered, walking faster.

Something reached up from the leaves and twigs beneath his feet and snagged his shoelace. He fell forward with a yelp and crashed to the ground. His flashlight bounced from his fingers into a patch of weeds, taking most of the light with it.

He ripped his shoelace free from the clawed root sticking out of the ground and scrambled up, leaving his flashlight where it fell. There was no time to dig it out.

He took off. The treasure box was heavy in his arms, the contents rattling, but he didn't slow down. He ran as fast and as far as his legs would carry him.

Holly waited for Jordan to come out and play the next morning. They usually met up at her house, but she decided to surprise him here instead of waiting. It always made him happy to know she was excited to spend time with him.

Holly crouched in the bushes, waiting for the right moment to jump out at her friend and make him squeak. He did that sometimes when she got him good.

She watched the front door of his house. What was taking him so long? They didn't bump into each other on the path in the woods, which meant he hadn't left yet.

The front door opened, and Sheriff Radcliffe stepped out. "I don't know where he is, Tammy, but I wouldn't worry."

Jordan's mom wrapped a sweater around herself and followed him onto the porch, her eyes darting around the yard. "He went out yesterday and didn't come back last night. Of course I'm worried. This isn't like him."

Holly shifted in the bushes, fear flapping around in her belly like frantic bats. Jordan didn't come home after he left the house last night? Holly had kept an eye on him for as long as she could, but what if something happened once he was deep in the woods?

"He could've gotten lost," Mrs. Radcliffe said. "We need to go look for him, Jed. There are predators in those woods. Something could've attacked him."

The sheriff placed his wide-brim hat on his head. "We're not going to waste hours of our lives looking for him. He'll find his own way back."

Anger fizzled like soda bubbles in Holly's stomach. How could he say that? Jordan was missing. He could've been grabbed by the sapling and dragged back to the watcher tree. What if all that was left him was a boot?

No, it can't have him, Holly thought, her fingers curling into fists. If Jordan got gulped down by the roots of that wicked tree, she would dig down and rescue him, and then she would chop that tree down. All by herself if she had to. Nothing was allowed to eat *her* best friend.

Holly blew the bangs from her eyes and started to crawl out of the bushes so she could race home and get a shovel, when a whisper came from behind her.

"Why are you hiding?"

She squeaked and fell forward in surprise. She whirled around to see Jordan crouched in the bushes too.

"Made you squeak," he said with a goofy grin.

Holly threw a chunk of dirt at him and huffed. "I thought you got lost or eaten by the watcher tree. Your mom said you didn't come back last night."

"I made it back before dark. She's talking about Patch, her cat. He ran out yesterday evening, but he'll come back eventually."

"Oh." Holly pushed herself up and brushed the dirt from her hands, feeling silly for worrying. "I had a plan to rescue you and everything."

Jordan's smile disappeared. "I thought I might need rescuing last night. I saw something scary in the woods."

Holly narrowed her eyes. Was he teasing her because she believed in the watcher tree and he didn't? "Something like what?"

"Like a big shape not too far from your house. And then my shoelace got caught on a root, and I fell. I ran away so fast my stomach hurt by the time I got home."

"What was it?"

"I don't know. It could've been an animal or a man. It was big like a man."

"But why would a man be in the woods near my house at night?" There was nothing around but trees.

Jordan shrugged. "I don't know. I don't really know what it was. All I care is it didn't get me."

"Don't worry. If anything ever gets you, I'll come rescue you."

"I'd come rescue you too."

"Promise?" Holly asked.

He made an *X* over his chest with a finger. "Cross my heart and hope to die. Let's go see if the treasure box belongs to Mr. Hallowell."

They crawled out of the bushes and headed for town.

The last house was as ordinary as could be—yellow and white with flowers in a rainbow of colors. They popped up all over with enough personality that they could be from Wonderland.

Jordan hooked his thumbs under the straps of his backpack, trying to ease some of the weight on his shoulders. He'd stuffed the box into his school backpack, but it was so big the zipper wouldn't close. He probably should've first taken out all the notebooks and junk he'd stuffed in there on the last day of school, but he didn't think about that this morning.

He studied the house. "What if this John isn't the right John either?"

He didn't want to haul this box around all day, trying to find the right person. He was sore after helping Mr. Cross, and his arms might fall off, and then there would be nothing to keep his backpack straps up.

Holly tapped a finger against her chin in thought. "We could go talk to the *bad* John. Mr. Berkshire said not to, but he's not the boss of us."

"I don't think that's a good idea."

"*Bad* could mean grumpy or rude."

"Or it means he's a lawbreaker. I told Mr. Berkshire I wouldn't take you there, and I won't." Even if she tried to boss him into it, he wouldn't do it. Mom was right—Holly didn't always understand when something was a bad idea.

Holly sighed. "Fine."

Jordan raised a hand to swat at a bumblebee bobbing past his face, but caught himself. If he hurt it out of fear or annoyance, Holly would be mad at him. And he didn't want her to be mad at him again.

"There's too many bees," he said instead.

Holly pointed at another bumblebee, this one coated in yellow pollen from the flower he'd been rolling around in. "He looks like a flying cheese puff."

"How do you know it's a boy bee?"

"Male bumbles don't have stingers," someone said, and a woman in a straw hat popped up from behind a flowering bush beside the house. She wiped the back of a dirty glove across her sweaty forehead, leaving a brown streak. "The queen and the female worker bees, the ones that collect pollen, are the ones with stingers. But they won't bother you if you don't bother them."

"You sure know a lot about bees," Jordan said, walking up the sidewalk with Holly.

"I love bees. They're important to our ecosystem, and I appreciate the honey they create. It makes good sweet tea in the summer."

"I like sweet tea," Holly said, then tilted her head. "Why are you pulling out the flowers?"

"These look like flowers, but they're actually weeds." The woman dropped a handful of them into a bucket beside her.

"Are you gonna smoke those weeds?"

Jordan smacked a hand against his forehead. Why did Holly ask her that?

The woman gave Holly a strange look. "Why would you ask that?"

"I heard people do that sometimes even though they're not supposed to."

Understanding shone on the woman's face. "Ah, I see. No, that wouldn't be good for me or most anyone else. These weeds are going into the garbage where they belong."

"But they belong in the ground where they grew. You pulled them out," Holly said, her tone challenging.

"You're right, but if I don't, they'll suck up the water and nutrients the flowers and bushes need, which could kill them, and the bees need the flowers to live and make honey."

Holly thought about that for a second, then said, "That makes sense. My mom doesn't pull weeds 'cause that's all we have. Weeds and grass and dirt. I like your flowers."

"Thank you." The woman removed her gloves. "What brings you two to my doorstep this afternoon?"

"We found your address in the phone book. What does the *J* stand for in Mr. J. Hallowell?" Holly asked.

"My husband's name is Joseph."

Disappointment added to the weight on Jordan's shoulders. "Are you sure it's not John?"

Amusement twinkled in the woman's eyes. "Am I sure my husband's name isn't John? Yes, I'm sure. Why are you two looking for this John Hallowell?"

"We don't know if we are, but we're looking for a John *something*. And he's really old, we think. Like eighty or ninety maybe," Jordan said.

"My father-in-law's name is John."

Holly gasped and blurted, "Did he grow up here? Is he really old? Does he still live here?"

Mrs. Hallowell laughed. "He's eighty-nine, and he did grow up here. He moved away for a while, but now he's back in town and living with us."

"Could we talk to him?" Jordan asked.

"Let me make sure he's feeling up to it." She stood and brushed the dirt from her knees. "Come have a seat on the porch before you get any more sunburned."

117

Holly rubbed the tip of her nose, which had started turning pink on the walk over, and followed the woman up the steps. She plopped into a rocking chair, and Jordan took the one beside her.

Jordan let his backpack slide to the porch between his feet and shrugged his aching shoulders. He dragged the huge metal box from the bag and into his lap.

Please let this be the right John, he thought.

Mrs. Hallowell pushed open the screen door, and a man, probably her husband, pushed an old man in a wheelchair out onto the porch.

The old man's knobby, wrinkled fingers—more like old tree branches than fingers—rested on a plaid blanket in his lap, and his blue eyes brightened with delight when he saw them. "What brings you two spring chickens to see an old man like me?"

Holly bristled. "I'm not a chicken."

"Oh, no offense intended, little Miss," Mr. Hallowell said, his voice crackling with old age. "Spring chicken refers to your young age, not how brave you are."

"Oh, well . . . that's okay, I guess."

Jordan slid off the rocking chair and carried the box over to the old man. "Is this yours?"

Mr. Hallowell drew in a breath and reached for it. "I never thought I would see this again. It's been . . . almost eighty years."

Jordan eased the box into the old man's lap.

Mr. Hallowell ran his fingers over it, tears beading his eyelashes. "Our initials were scratched into the lid right here, beneath this patch of rust. Mine and Elias's."

"Who's Elias?" Holly asked.

"He was my best friend when I was a boy. Closer than a brother. This box belonged to my father before me. He was discharged from the war after he was injured, and this old ammunition box came home with him, filled with his belongings. It was a painful reminder for him, so he threw it out. I rescued it from the garbage, and it became mine and Elias's treasure box. I looked for this for years, but I never knew where he buried it."

"We found it buried by the watcher tree," Holly said, climbing out of her chair.

Mr. Hallowell looked up in surprise. "And you two brave souls dug it up?"

"It's only an old tree," Jordan told him.

"Elias and I never believed the stories either. There was a little boy who disappeared when my grandmother was younger, and all they found of him was a boot near an old tree with a haunting face. That's when the legend of the watcher tree began."

Holly planted her hands on her hips. "Is it true the tree ate him, or is it just a spooky story?"

"My grandmother believed the boy ran away from home because his family treated him terribly. He left a bloody boot by the roots of that tree to make everyone think wild animals had gotten him. If they believed he was

119

dead, they wouldn't look for him. And no one did. He simply . . . disappeared."

"Does that mean the tree's not alive?" Holly asked.

"It's alive, but that old tree has more in common with a flower than a hungry wolf that hunts at night. Of course, that's just one old man's opinion."

Jordan glanced at Holly, who seemed unsure whether or not Mr. Hallowell's version of the story was true. Jordan believed him. It made more sense than a man-eating tree. "Why did your friend pick that spot?"

"I expect he buried it there because everyone else was afraid to go near that tree, but also as a dare. Would I be courageous enough to dig near the roots of the legendary man-eating tree? Sadly, I looked everywhere *but* there."

"Why bury it?" Holly asked.

"The best kind of treasure is buried, my dear."

Holly and Jordan exchanged a grin. There weren't many adults who thought like they did.

"We would take turns filling this box with interesting items, and then we would make maps and clues for each other," Mr. Hallowell explained. "It was great fun."

"You couldn't read the map he gave you? Is that why you couldn't find it?" Holly asked. "I'm not good at reading maps either."

"Elias never had a chance to make the map." Sadness touched his voice. "The Spanish flu was a problem that year, and he got sick."

"Oh no," Holly said. "He didn't die, did he?"

Mr. Hallowell lowered his head. "I'm afraid so."

Holly puckered her lips between her teeth, her eyes shinier than usual. It bothered her when other people were sad or hurting, like she could feel what they felt. Jordan thought about asking Mr. Hallowell to stop telling his story before the details could make her feel worse, but he was curious to know the rest of it.

Jordan stepped closer to Holly, raised an arm, hesitated, and then awkwardly wrapped it around her shoulders—the way Mom did when *he* was sad. He didn't know if it would make her feel better or not, but he hoped so.

She moved closer, leaning against him.

"While Elias had the box, he told me he was making something special for me. He never did tell me what it was, and once he got sick, I wasn't allowed to see him. Everyone was afraid of the sickness spreading," Mr. Hallowell continued.

Jordan couldn't imagine not being able to see his friends if they got really sick. It was hard enough not seeing Holly and Gin for a few days because they caught a stomach bug.

Mr. Hallowell opened the box and studied the contents. He picked up the rolled paper and smiled at the unreadable message. "Written in our special code. We were the only two who could read it. It says, 'Brother, I've carved a gift for you. Finding it required courage, and you deserve it even more now.'"

He set down the note and picked up the wooden bear. Fresh tears brightened his eyes. "I loved bears. I told Elias I wished I could have a pet bear, but my father said bears weren't meant to be pets." His lips quivered. "He made this for me. I saw him working on it before it had taken much shape, but he wouldn't tell me what it was."

"You all right, Pop?" Joseph Hallowell asked, touching his father's shoulder.

"Fine, fine. Remembering my friend, that's all." Mr. Hallowell sighed and picked up the golden bullet with his other hand. "We found this rifle cartridge in the woods one day, and as I was bending down to pick it up, we heard a gunshot. A hunter with bad eyesight mistook us for deer. Bending down to pick up this stray cartridge saved my life that day. I assume a hunter dropped it while loading his rifle and lost sight of it. I never really believed in luck, but God used this little thing to save my life that day." He stared at it in the palm of his hand and then held it out to Jordan. "A reminder for you that God is always watching over us."

"Really? For me?" Jordan took it. It had been a boring bullet before, but now—with the story behind it and the fact that it was a gift—it felt special. "Thanks, Mr. Hallowell."

"You're welcome." He picked up the harmonica next. "My family was poorer than Elias's, and they couldn't afford to buy me the harmonica I wanted. Elias said he would lend me his and teach me how to play." He smoothed his fingers over the harmonica. "This should be with someone who has a big heart and a passionate soul, and I think I know the perfect person." He offered it to Holly.

"But your friend wanted you to have it."

"These old lungs couldn't play it now. It should be with someone who can enjoy it. There might still be a powerful spark of friendship in that harmonica, and you never know what might happen when you play it."

Was he trying to say it *was* magic? Jordan thought back to the flickering lights and blown lightbulb at the Inn. No way . . .

"The marble is new." Mr. Hallowell studied the glass ball pinched between his thumb and finger. "It must've been something he found." He set it aside and removed the rock hard Tootsie Roll from the box. "This was our favorite candy. I guess it's a little too hard to eat now."

Holly fished a quarter from her pocket and held it out. "The gnome lady gave me this for candy yesterday, but you can have it to buy another Tootsie Roll. Since it's your favorite."

Mr. Hallowell smiled. "It's sweet of you to offer, but between you and me . . ."—he cupped a hand around his mouth and leaned forward to whisper—"I have a whole bag of Tootsie Rolls stashed in the toaster in the lower cupboard. You keep your quarter for you."

Holly grinned. "Good hiding spot."

Mr. Hallowell leaned back in his chair and looked at Jordan and Holly. "Thank you for finding this and bringing it to me. To most people, this would look like a box of junk, but it's special to me."

"We're glad you have it back," Jordan said. "And Holly and I didn't have that hard of a time finding you."

"We had to get past the angry dog, the old guy with a bad heart, and the gnome lady who isn't a witch," Holly explained.

"That sounds like quite an adventure. You'll have to come back and tell it to me sometime."

"Is it really okay if we come back and visit?" Holly asked. "You're kind of like the grandpas I see on TV, but I don't have a grandpa to tell me cool stories."

"Oh, little one." He reached over and took Holly's hand. "You come back and visit me anytime. I have all kinds of stories to share. And sugary sweets I'm not supposed to have at my age." He winked, and Holly grinned. "You can bring the harmonica and play me some music."

"I don't think that would be good for your lightbulbs," Jordan mumbled.

Holly lifted her chin. "I exploded one."

"How interesting."

"I think it's time to rest, Pop." Joseph Hallowell patted his dad on the shoulders. "Doctors orders and all that."

"All right. It has been a pleasure meeting both of you," Mr. Hallowell said. "I hope you know how special it is to have a best friend. You two hold on to each other."

"Yes, sir," Jordan said. "It was nice meeting you too."

Holly gave the old man a hug and then bounced down the steps to the sidewalk. Jordan thought about Mr. Hallowell's words as he followed her. It *was* special having a best friend. He knew other kids who didn't have one. He was lucky. "Blessed," Oma would say. And maybe that was better.

He was blessed to have a best friend to go on this adventure with. They had solved the mystery of John and his buried treasure all on their own. There was no telling where the next mystery might take them.

Keep an eye out for the next installment of
MYSTERIES, MISCHIEF, and MARSHMALLOWS

About the Author

Jesus and laughter have brought C.C. Warrens through some very difficult times in life, and she weaves both into every story she writes, creating a world of breath-stealing intensity, laugh-out-loud humor, and a sparkle of hope. Writing has been a slowly blossoming dream inside her for most of her life until one day it spilled out onto the pages that would become her first published book.

If she's not writing, she's attempting to bake something—however catastrophic that might be—or she's enjoying the beauty of the outdoors with her husband.

CONTACT
Facebook: ccwarrens
Instagram: c.c._warrens
TikTok: c.c._warrens
Website: ccwarrens.com